BETTER THINK TWICE ABOUT IT

BETTER THINK TWICE
ABOUT IT

And Twelve Other Stories

by

LUIGI PIRANDELLO

Nobel Prize Winner In Literature, 1934

Translated by

ARTHUR AND HENRIE MAYNE

NEW YORK
E. P. DUTTON & CO., INC.

FIRST PRINTING . . . . NOVEMBER, 1934
SECOND PRINTING . . . NOVEMBER, 1934

CONTENTS

c.1

THE OTHER SON

THE OTHER SON

"IS Ninfarosa in?"

"Yes, knock at the door."

Old Maragrazia gave a knock and settled herself down quietly on the rickety steps in front of the door.

Those steps were her natural seat—those and many other front-door steps—for she spent her time sitting huddled before the door-way of one or other of the cottages of Farnia, either asleep or dissolved in silent tears. When a passer-by threw a copper or a piece of bread into her lap, she scarcely roused herself from her sleep or dried her tears: she kissed the copper or the bread, crossed herself and continued weeping or dozing.

She was a bundle of rags—thick, greasy rags—always the same, in summer or winter, tattered, torn and faded, and stinking foully of sweat and the filth of the streets. Her sallow face was covered with a close network of wrinkles and her eyelids gaped open, bloody and horrible, inflamed by the incessant flow of her tears. But from between those wrinkles, through the blood and tears, there

1

shone a pair of bright eyes—eyes that seemed to peer out across a great distance—the eyes of a long-forgotten childhood. The flies settled hungrily on those eyes, but she remained so deeply absorbed in her sorrow that she did not drive them away or so much as notice them. Her dry and scanty hair was parted on the top of her head and ended in two matted locks hanging above her ears, whose lobes were torn by the weight of the massive ear-rings she had worn in her youth. A deep black furrow started at her chin and ran down her flabby throat, until it disappeared in her hollow breast.

The women sitting at their thresholds paid no attention to her any more. They spent almost the whole day there, chatting in front of their cottages—some patching clothing, others preparing veget-ables or knitting, all occupied with some task. The dwellings were house and stable combined, lighted only by the door-way, and paved with cobble-stones the same as the streets. On one side was the manger, with an ass or a mule, kicking to keep off the persistent flies; on the other side was the bed, towering up like a monument. Each room con-tained also a long black chest of pine or beech-wood, which looked as if it were a coffin, two or three straw-bottomed chairs, a kneading trough and some agricultural implements. The rough and sooty walls were decorated with a few common halfpenny prints, representing the particular saints dear to that countryside. In the street, which reeked with smoke and manure, sun-burnt children played—some stark naked, others in little dirty, tattered shirts. Hens scratched about among the children; young pigs, caked in mud, sniffed and grunted, digging into the heaps of garbage.

That day, the women were discussing the latest party of emigrants which was to leave the next morning for South America.

"Saro Scoma is going," said one of them. "He's leaving behind him his wife and three children."

"Vito Scordia," added another, "leaves five and his wife, who is pregnant."

"Is it true," asked a third, "that Carmine Ronca is taking his twelve-year-old son who had already started working in the sulphur mines? Blessed Virgin! he might at least have left the boy with his wife. How will that poor woman manage for help now?"

"How they cried all night long in the house of Nunzio Ligreci . . ." called out a fourth woman in pitiful tones from farther up the street. "What tears they've shed—Nunzio's son, Nico, who's only just returned from his military service, has decided to go too."

At this piece of news, old Maragrazia pressed her shawl over her mouth to prevent an outburst of sobbing, but the vehemence of her grief caused an endless flow of tears to well up from her inflamed eyes.

Fourteen years before, her two sons had also left for America. They had promised to return after four or five years, but they had prospered there—especially the elder one—and they had forgotten their old mother. Every time a fresh body of emigrants was to leave Farnia, she went to Ninfarosa to get her to write a letter for her, and begged some member of the party to be so kind as to deliver it personally to one or other of those two sons. Then, as the party of emigrants—heavily laden with sacks and bundles—set out for the nearest railway station, the old woman joined with the mothers, wives and sisters who, with tears and cries of despair, followed after along the dusty highroad. As she walked, on one of these occasions, she gazed steadily at the eyes of a young emigrant, who was making a great show of noisy cheerfulness, in order to discourage manifestations of grief from the relations who accompanied him.

"Mad old crone!" he shouted at her. "Why are you looking at me like that? D'you want to make my eyes drop out?"

"No, my fine fellow! I envy you those eyes, because, with them, you'll see my sons. Tell them the state I was in when you left here, and say that if they delay any longer they won't find me alive. . . ."

4

THE OTHER SON

The gossips of the neighbourhood were still going through the list of those who were leaving the next day. Near by, an old man lay on his back in the lane, his head pillowed on a donkey's saddle, listening to the chatter and quietly smoking his pipe. Suddenly he folded his great horny hands across his chest, spat and said:—

"If I were king, I should not allow one single letter to be sent from over there to Farnia any more."

"Three cheers for Jaco Spina!" exclaimed one of the women. "And how would the poor mothers and wives manage without any news or help?"

"They send too many letters—that's the trouble," the old man muttered, and spat again. "The mothers could go into service and the wives could go to the bad. . . . Why don't those fellows mention in their letters the hardships they find over there? They only describe the good side of things, and every letter that comes calls up these ignorant lads and carries them off. Where are the hands for working our fields? At Farnia, the only people left are old men, women and babies. I've got some land and I have to watch it going to ruin. What can I do with only a single pair of hands? And still they go and still they go! Rain on their faces and wind on their backs, say I. I hope they'll break their necks, the damned fools!"

BETTER THINK TWICE ABOUT IT

At that moment Ninfarosa opened her door. It was as if the sun had suddenly appeared in the little street. She was dark, with rich colouring, sparkling black eyes and bright red lips. Her form was slender but strong, and she exhaled a kind of wild gaiety. A large red and yellow spotted handkerchief was knotted over her shapely bosom and in her ears were thick golden rings. Her hair was black and curling, and she wore it drawn back without a parting, fastened on to the nape of her neck in a shining coil wound round a silver dagger. A deep dimple in the middle of her wellrounded chin gave her a humorous look and added still further to her fascinations.

Left a widow after barely two years of marriage, Ninfarosa had been deserted by her second husband, who had gone to America five years ago. No one was supposed to know it, but, at night, one of the leading residents of the village visited her, entering through the orchard and the back door. And therefore the neighbours—who were respectable, Godfearing women—looked askance at her, while they secretly envied her luck. They had another grudge against her, for it was said in the village that, out of revenge for being deserted by her second husband, she had written several anonymous letters to the emigrants in America, making slanderous charges against some of the unfortunate women.

"Who's that preaching?" she asked, coming out into the lane. "Oh, it's Jaco Spina! It would be much better, Uncle Jaco, if only we women remained at Farnia. We'd cultivate the fields."

"You women," the old man muttered in husky tones—"You women are only good for one thing." And he spat.

"For what thing, Uncle Jaco? Go on, say it."

"For weeping—and for one other thing."

"Ah! That makes two things then. I do not weep, you see."

"Yes, I know that, my girl. You didn't even weep when your first husband died!"

"But if I had died first, Uncle Jaco," retorted Ninfarosa promptly, "d'you think he wouldn't have taken another wife? Of course he would! But look here—see who weeps enough for all of us—Maragrazia."

"That depends," murmured Jaco Spina, stretch‚ ing himself out again on his back. "Since the old woman has water to get rid of, she gets rid of it from her eyes too."

The women laughed. Roused from her abstrac‚ tion, Maragrazia cried:—

"I have lost two sons, handsome as the sun, and you would not have me weep?"

"Handsome indeed! Yes, very handsome, and worth weeping over—" said Ninfarosa. "There they are over there, swimming in abundance, and they leave you here to die—a beggar."

"They are the sons and I am their mother," replied the old woman. "How can they realise my grief?"

"Well, I don't know the reason for so many tears and all this grief," replied Ninfarosa, "when it was you yourself—people say—who worried them and plagued them until they went off."

"I?" exclaimed Maragrazia, utterly amazed. Beating her fist against her chest, she rose to her feet. "I? Who said so?"

"Somebody or other said it."

"A shame! A shame on them—I? My sons? I who . . ."

"Oh, don't mind her!" interrupted one of the women. "Can't you see she's joking?"

Ninfarosa indulged in a long laugh, swaying her body contemptuously from the hips; then, to make up to the old woman for her cruel jest, she asked in a kindly tone:—

"Well, well, Granny, what is it you want?"

Maragrazia put a shaky hand to her bosom and pulled out a badly crumpled sheet of paper and an envelope. She showed them to Ninfarosa with a look of entreaty.

"If you would do me the usual favour. . . ."

"What? Another letter?"

"If you would be so good. . . ."

THE OTHER SON

Ninfarosa sniffed; then, knowing that it would be impossible to get rid of the old woman, she invited her into her house.

This house was not like the others in that neigh-bourhood. The large room was rather dark when the door was shut, because its only other light was from a grated window above the door, but it was a white-washed room with a brick floor, and all was clean and well-kept. There was an iron bed-stead, a wardrobe, a marble-topped chest of drawers and a small inlaid walnut table—humble furniture, it is true, but clearly Ninfarosa could not have afforded the luxury of purchasing it herself, out of the very uncertain income she earned as a village dress-maker.

She took her pen and inkstand, placed the crumpled sheet of paper on the top of the high chest of drawers and prepared to write, standing up.

"Be quick, out with it!"

" *'Dear sons'*," the old woman began to dictate.

" *'I have no longer any eyes to weep with. . . .'*," continued Ninfarosa, with a weary sigh. She knew the usual formula for these letters.

The old woman added:—

" *'Because my eyes are inflamed by the longing to see you at least for one last time. . . .'*."

"Get on, get on!" urged Ninfarosa. "You must have written that to them quite thirty times, at the very least."

9

"Well, you write it. It's the truth, my dear, don't you see? So now write: *'Dear sons'. . . .*"

"What? All over again?"

"No. This time it's something different. I thought it out all last night. Listen: *'Dear sons: Your poor old mother promises and vows'*—yes, like that—*'promises and vows before God, that if you return to Farnia, she will make over to you, during her life-time, her cottage'*."

Ninfarosa burst out laughing. "That cottage! But since they're already so rich, what d'you expect them to do with your four walls of wattles plastered with mud? Why, they'd collapse if one blew on them!"

"Well, you write it," repeated the old woman obstinately. "Four rough bits of stone in one's own country are worth more than a whole kingdom outside. Write it, write."

"I have written it. What else would you like to add?"

"Just this—*'that your poor Mamma, dear sons, shivers from the cold now that the winter is starting. She would like to have some kind of a dress made but cannot afford to do so; would you be so kind as to send her at least a bank note for five lire, so that'* . . ."

"Enough, enough, enough!" said Ninfarosa, folding up the sheet and putting it into the en-velope. "I've written it good and proper. That's enough."

"Also about the five lire?" asked the old woman, surprised at the unexpected speed with which it had been finished.

"Yes, yes, everything, also about the five lire, my Lady."

"Written it properly? Everything?"

"Ouf! Yes, I tell you."

"Be patient . . . be a little patient with this poor old woman, my daughter," said Maragrazia. "What can you expect of me? I am half stupid nowadays. . . . May God and his beauteous and most holy Mother requite you for the favour."

She took the letter and placed it in her bosom. She had decided to entrust it to the son of Nunzio Ligreci, who was leaving for Rosario in Santa Fe, where her sons were. She went off to find him.

* * * * *

By evening, the women had gone back into their cottages and almost all the doors were shut. Not a soul was to be seen in the narrow lanes, except the lamp/lighter going his rounds, ladder on shoulder, to light the few small kerosene/oil lamps, whose sparse and feeble glimmer gave a still more gloomy aspect to those silent, deserted ill/kept alleys.

Old Maragrazia walked along, stooping low. With one hand she pressed the letter to her bosom, as if she hoped to transmit to that piece of paper the warmth of a mother's love. She employed the other hand in frequent scratching of her back and head. With each fresh letter, hope revived strongly within her—hope that at last she would succeed in touching the hearts of her sons—in calling them back to her. Surely when they read her words, eloquent of all the tears which she had shed for them during the past fourteen years, her handsome sons, her sweet sons would be unable to stand out against her entreaties any longer. . . .

But on this occasion, as it happened, she was not thoroughly satisfied with the letter which she carried in her bosom. It seemed to her as if Nin* farosa had dashed it off too hurriedly and she did not feel at all sure that she had put in the last part properly—the part about the five lire for the dress. Five lire! Surely it would mean nothing to her sons—her rich sons—to pay five lire for cloth* ing for their old mother, who suffered so dreadfully from the cold. . . .

Meanwhile, from behind the closed doors of the cottages, there came the sound of weeping—mothers weeping for the sons who would leave them in the morning.

"Oh! sons, sons," groaned Maragrazia to herself, pressing the letter more firmly to her breast—"How can you have the heart to go? You promise to return and you do not come. . . . Ah, poor old women, do not trust their promises! Your

12

sons, like mine, will never come back . . . they
will never come back. . . ."

Suddenly, she stopped beneath a lamp-post, hearing footsteps in the lane. Who was that?

Ah! It was the new parish-doctor—that young
man who had recently come and who, they said,
would soon be leaving, not because he had failed
to do good work, but because he was in the black
books of the few big gentlefolk of the village. The
poor, on the other hand, had all taken to him at
once. He was only a boy to look at, but he was an
old man, as far as sense and learning went. People
said that he, too, meant to leave for America. But
then he no longer had a mother—no, he was alone.

"Doctor," asked Maragrazia, "would you do me
a favour?"

The young doctor stopped under the lamp-post,
taken by surprise. Walking along, deep in thought,
he had not noticed the old woman.

"Who are you? Oh, you are . . . Yes, of
course, you're . . ."

He remembered then that he had seen that
bundle of rags on several occasions in front of some
cottage door.

"Would you do me the favour, Doctor, of reading me this little letter, which I have to send to my
sons."

"If I can see to read it," said the doctor, who was
short-sighted. He settled his glasses on his nose.

13

BETTER THINK TWICE ABOUT IT

Maragrazia drew the letter from her bosom, held it out and waited in expectation that he would begin to read the words dictated to Ninfarosa—"Dear sons"—but no! either the doctor could not see to read the writing, or he was unable to decipher it.

He put the paper close to his eyes, moved it away to get more light on it from the street lamp, turned it over from one side to the other, and finally said:

"But what is this?"

"Can't you read it, your Honour?" enquired Maragrazia timidly.

The doctor started laughing.

"But there's nothing to read—there's nothing written on it," he said. "Four scrawls, drawn down zigzag with the pen. Here, you look at it."

"What!" exclaimed the old woman in conster‹ nation.

"It is so. Just look! Nothing! There's nothing written down at all."

"Is it possible!" cried the old woman. "How? Why, I dictated it to her, to Ninfarosa, word by word, and I saw her write."

"She must have pretended to, then," said the doctor, shrugging his shoulders.

Maragrazia remained a moment as if petrified. Then, giving herself a violent blow on the chest, she broke out in a torrent of words:—

"Ah! the wretch! The vile wretch! Why did

14

she deceive me? So that's why my sons don't send me any answer. They've never had a line from me. . . . She's never written anything of what I dictated. . . . That's the reason! So my sons know nothing of my condition—they don't know that I'm at death's door through pining for them. . . . And I was blaming them, Doctor, whilst all the time it was she—that vile wretch there—who's been making a mockery of me! My God! my God! How *could* anyone behave so treacherously to a poor mother, to a poor old woman like me? Oh! what a thing to do . . . what a thing to do. . . . Oh!——"

The young doctor was full of sympathy and indignation, and tried to comfort her in her distress. He made her tell him who Ninfarosa was and where her cottage was, so that next day he could give her the scolding she deserved. But the old woman still went on excusing her absent sons for their long silence; she was overcome with remorse to think that she had blamed them during so many years for deserting her. She was quite convinced now that they would have returned, would have hastened back to her, if a single one of the many letters which she had believed she had sent had really been written and had reached them.

To cut the scene short, the doctor had to promise that he would write the sons a long letter on the following morning.

"Come, come, don't despair like that! Come to me in the morning. Not now—it's time to sleep. Come in the morning. Go to sleep now."

But it was no use—about two hours later, when the doctor passed back along the lane, he found her still there, weeping inconsolably as she squatted under the lamp-post. He scolded her, made her get up and told her to go straight home, at once, as it was now very late.

"Where do you live?"

"Ah! Doctor. . . . I have a cottage down there, at the end of the village. I told that vile wretch to write to my sons that I would make it over to them during my life-time if they would only return. She started laughing—the hussy—because it is nothing but four walls of wattle plastered with mud, she said. But I——"

"Very well, very well," the doctor cut her short again. "You go to bed now, and to-morrow we'll write about the cottage also. Come along, I'll accompany you."

"God bless your Excellency! But what are you saying, Doctor? Accompany me? No, your Honour, you go on in front. I'm a poor old woman and I walk slowly."

The doctor said good-night to her and went off. Maragrazia followed him at a distance. When she reached the door where she had seen him go in, she stopped, pulled her shawl over her head, wrapped

16

it well round her and sat down on the steps in front of the door, to spend the night there, waiting.

At dawn she was asleep when the doctor, an early riser, came out for his first round of visits. As he opened his door, the old woman rolled over at his feet, for she had gone to sleep leaning against it.

"Good heavens! Is that you? Are you hurt?"

"No. . . . Your Honour pardon me . . ." she stammered, struggling to her feet with difficulty, for her hands and arms were still enveloped in the shawl.

"Have you spent the night here?"

"Yes, Sir. . . . It's nothing; I'm used to it . . ." the old woman said, excusing herself. "What can you expect, young gentleman? I cannot keep calm. . . . I cannot keep calm after the treachery of that wretch. . . . I should like to kill her, Doctor! She might have told me that she found it a nuisance writing for me, and I should have gone to someone else. I could have come to your Honour, who is so kind. . . ."

"Yes, yes, you wait here a little," said the doctor, "I'm going now to that good woman. Then we will write the letter. Just wait."

And he hurried away in the direction the old woman had pointed out the night before.

When he asked a woman in the lane which was

17

Ninfarosa's house, he discovered that it was Ninfarosa herself to whom he was speaking.

"Here I am, I'm the person you want, Doctor,"
she said with a smile and a blush, and asked him to
come in.

She had seen him pass by on several occasions—
that nice, boyish-looking doctor. As she was
always in good health herself and not able to
pretend that she was ill, there was no excuse for
calling him in. She was delighted, therefore, at his
visit, though rather surprised that he had come of
his own accord to speak to her. As soon as she
knew the reason for his call and saw that he was
worried and annoyed, she assumed a submissive,
but seductive, air. Her expression showed how
grieved she was at his displeasure—his quite un-
justifiable displeasure. The moment she could get
a word in, without being so ill-bred as to interrupt
him, she began:—

"I beg your pardon, Doctor,"—and as she spoke
she half closed her handsome dark eyes, "but are
you seriously upset because of that old madwoman?
Here in the village everyone knows her, Doctor,
and no one pays any attention to her now. Ask
anybody you like and they'll all tell you she's mad,
quite mad, for the past fourteen years, ever since
her two sons left for America. She will not admit
that they've forgotten all about her—which is the
truth—but persists in writing, again and again.

Well, just to satisfy her—you understand—I make a pretence of writing a letter for her; then those who are leaving pretend that they will deliver it, and she, poor woman, is taken in. Why, if everyone behaved the way she does, my dear Doctor, the world would be in a pretty state. Look here, I also have been deserted—deserted by my husband. Yes, Doctor! And d'you know what cheek the fine gentleman had? He sent me a portrait of himself and his girl over there! I can show it to you. They were taken with their heads resting one against the other and their hands clasped—allow me, give me your hand—like this, d'you understand? And they're smiling, smiling in the face of whoever looks at them—that is in my face, if you please! Ah, Doctor . . . all the pity is lavished on those who go, and none on those who stay behind. I have wept too, you see, in the early days. Then I pulled myself together and now—now I manage to get along and I enjoy myself too, when I get the chance, seeing that the world is made the way it is. . . ."

The young doctor was becoming quite nervous, overwhelmed by the fascinating friendliness and sympathy of this handsome creature. He lowered his eyes and said:—

"But—you perhaps have enough to live on, while that poor woman, on the other hand——"

"What? She?" cried Ninfarosa vivaciously.

19

"She could have enough to live on, too, if she wished—well prepared and put into her mouth—only she doesn't wish it."

"What?" asked the doctor, looking up again in surprise.

Ninfarosa burst out laughing at the expression of amazement on his handsome face. Her beautiful smile revealed a set of strong, white teeth.

"Yes, indeed!" she said. "She doesn't wish it. She has another son—the youngest—who would like her to live with him and would see that she lacked nothing."

"Another son? That old woman?"

"Yes, Sir. He's called Rocco Trupia. She won't have anything to do with him."

"But why?"

"Because she's quite mad—haven't I told you? She weeps day and night for those who have deserted her, and she won't accept even a crust of bread from the other son, who clasps his hands and implores her. . . . She takes from strangers—yes. Not from him."

Unwilling to display further astonishment and anxious to conceal his increasing nervousness, the doctor frowned and said:—

"Perhaps he's treated her badly—the other son."

"I don't think so," said Ninfarosa. "He's a rough man, I admit, and always on the grumble, but he's not bad at heart. He is a worker, you see—

work, wife and children are the only interests he has. If your Honour would like to satisfy your curiosity, you haven't far to go. Look, follow this road for nearly a quarter of a mile, and just outside the village, on the left, you'll find what's called the 'House of the Column'. That's his place. He's rented a fine field, which brings him in a good return. Go there and you will see that the facts are as I tell you."

The doctor rose; the conversation had excited him and the balmy air of the September morning added to his cheerfulness. More interested than ever in the old woman's case, he said:—

"I am certainly going."

Ninfarosa put her hands behind her neck to readjust the coil of hair about the silver dagger; with an invitation in her half-closed smiling eyes, she replied:—

"A pleasant walk then. I am always at your service."

After mounting the steep slope, the doctor paused to regain his breath. There were a few poor cottages on either side and then the village ended. The lane came out on the provincial highway which ran dead straight and deep in dust for more than a mile along the wide plateau. The road was bordered by fields, most of which had been cropped with grain and were now a mass of yellow stubble. On the left, a splendid solitary

21

pine tree, looking like a gigantic umbrella, formed the goal of the young gentlemen of Farnia in their usual afternoon stroll. At the very end of the plateau rose a long range of bluish mountains, behind which dense white clouds, that looked like cotton-wool, lurked as if in ambush. Every now and then, one of them would leave the others and travel slowly across the sky, passing over Monte Mirotta, which rose behind Farnia. During its passage, the mountain below it was wrapped in a sombre purple shadow, then suddenly brightened again. The deep silence of the morning was broken from time to time by the sound of shots; the larks were just arriving, and peasants were shooting at them and at the turtle-doves as they passed over the plain; each shot was followed by a long and savage outburst of barking from the watch-dogs.

The doctor walked briskly along the road, looking around him at the dry fields which lay waiting to be ploughed as soon as the first showers had fallen. Farm-hands were scarce, however, and the whole country-side presented a sadly neglected appearance.

He perceived below him the 'House of the Column', so-called because one corner was upheld by the column of an ancient Greek temple, broken off at the top and badly worn away. The house was really only a wretched hovel—a 'roba' as the

Sicilian peasants call their rural dwellings. It was screened at the back by a thick hedge of cactus and in front of it stood a couple of large conical straw-ricks.

. "Ho there! Anyone in the *roba?*" shouted the doctor, who was afraid of dogs; so he waited in front of a small rickety gate of rusted iron.

A well-grown boy of about ten appeared; he was bare-footed, with a tousled mop of reddish hair, faded from the sun. He had the greenish eyes of a young wild animal.

"Is there a dog here?" the doctor asked.

"Yes, but he won't do anything; he's quite quiet."

"Are you Rocco Trupia's son?"

"Yes, Sir."

"Where is your father?"

"He's over there, unloading the manure from the mules."

The boy's mother sat on the wall in front of the *roba*. She was combing the hair of her eldest child, a girl of about twelve, who was sitting on an over-turned iron pail with her baby brother, a few months old, in her lap. Another small urchin was rolling about the ground among the hens, who showed no fear of him; the handsome cock, how-ever, had taken offence and was stretching out his neck and shaking his crest with annoyance.

"I should like to speak to Rocco Trupia," the

23

young doctor called to the woman. "I am the new parish doctor."

She remained a moment staring at him, worried, unable to think what business a doctor could have with her husband. She had been suckling the baby and her bodice was still open: she pushed her coarse shirt inside, did up the buttons, and rose to get a chair for her visitor. He declined the offer, however, and stood petting the child on the ground, while the other lad ran off to summon his father.

A few minutes later, there was the scraping sound of heavy, hob nailed boots, and Rocco Trupia appeared from among the cactus plants. He had long bow legs and walked with a stoop, one hand held behind his back, in the usual manner of the peasants.

His large, flat nose and the excessive length of his upper lip, clean shaven and up turned, gave him a simian look: he was red haired and his pale face was dotted with moles; from his deep sunk, greenish eyes flashed side long, shifty glances.

He greeted the doctor by raising his hand and pushing his black knitted cap slightly back from his forehead:

"I kiss your Honour's hand. What are your orders?"

"It's this way," began the doctor. "I have come to speak to you about your mother."

Rocco Trupia changed countenance.

"Is she ill?"

"No," the doctor hastened to add. "She is in her usual condition; but she's so old, you see, old and ragged and neglected. . . ."

Whilst the doctor was speaking, Rocco Trupia's agitation increased, until at last he could restrain himself no longer.

"Have you any other orders to give me, Doctor? I am at your service. But if your Honour has come to speak to me about my mother, you must excuse my saying good-bye to you and returning to my work."

"Wait! I know that it's not your fault that she is in want," said the doctor, trying to stop him from going. "I have been told that you even——"

"Come here, Doctor." Rocco Trupia pointed suddenly to the door of the *roba*. "It's only a poor man's house, but if your Honour is a village doctor, you must have seen many that are no better. I want to show you the bed always ready—you see—always prepared for that . . . good old woman. She is my mother, so I cannot speak of her in other terms. Here are my wife and children, who can assure you that I have always ordered them to serve that old woman and to respect her as they would the Blessed Virgin. For one's mother must be held sacred, Doctor. What have I done to that mother of mine that she should put me to such

25

shame before the whole village and make people think God only knows what of me. . . . It's true that from my babyhood I was brought up in the home of my father's people and that I have no call to respect her as a mother, because she has always been cold towards me. Yet I have respected her and wished her well. When those wretched sons of hers left her for America I hastened to her, to bring her here as mistress of my house. No, your Honour! She must play the beggar-woman in the village, make an exhibition of herself and bring disgrace upon me. I swear to you, Doctor, that if one of those wretched sons of hers returns to Farnia, I will kill him for the disgrace and the bitterness I've endured these past fourteen years on their account. . . . I will kill him, as true as I stand here talking to you in the presence of my wife and these four little ones. . . ."

Rocco Trupia was shaking with rage. His face had grown paler, his eyes were bloodshot, and he passed his hand across his mouth to wipe the foam off his lips.

The young doctor stood looking at him with indignation. "I see," he said, after a pause. "So that's why your mother refuses to accept the hospitality you offer. It's because of the hatred you foster against your brothers. That's clear."

"Hatred?" exclaimed Rocco Trupia, clenching his fist and bringing it out from behind his back.

"Yes, hatred *now*, Doctor. I hate them because they've caused so much suffering to my mother and to me. In the old days, when they were here, I loved them and looked up to them like elder brothers. And they, in return for it, behaved like Cain towards me. Just listen, Doctor. They would not work and I worked for the lot of us. They used to come here and tell me there was nothing to cook that evening and that mother would go supperless to bed, and I gave. . . . They got drunk, they squandered money on low women, and I gave. . . . When they left for America, I bled myself white for them—here is my wife who can tell you about it."

"Then why?" repeated the doctor, almost to himself.

Rocco Trupia gave a wry smile.

"Why? Because my mother says that I'm not her son."

"What?"

"Get her to explain it to you, Doctor. I have no time to lose; the men are waiting over there for me with the mules laden with manure. I have to work. . . . I can't bear to talk of it. Get her to tell you about it. I kiss your hands."

And Rocco Trupia went away as he had come, stooping, his long legs bowed, and one hand held to his back. The doctor's glance followed him for a moment, then he turned to look at the little ones who were mute with fright. He saw the wife clasp her hands together as she closed her eyes in her distress and said with a sigh of resignation:—

"We must leave it in God's hands."

* * * * *

On his return to the village, the doctor was still more anxious to get to the bottom of that strange and incredible case. The old woman was there, seated on the steps in front of his door, just as he had left her. He spoke rather sharply to her when telling her to come in.

"I have been to have a talk with your son at the 'House of the Column'," he said. "Why did you conceal from me the fact that you have another son here?"

Maragrazia looked at him, first in confusion, then almost in terror. Passing her shaking hand across her forehead and hair, she replied:—

"Oh, young Sir, I get into a cold sweat if your Honour speaks to me of that son. Please don't mention him to me, for pity's sake."

"Why not?" asked the doctor angrily. "What has he done to you? Speak out!"

"He has done nothing," the old woman hastened to answer. "That I must give him credit for, in all conscience. On the contrary, he has always behaved respectfully to me. But I . . . I . . . do you see how I tremble, my dear young Sir, as soon as I speak of it? I cannot speak of it! It's because—because—that man—is not my son, Doctor!"

The young practitioner lost his patience.

"What do you mean—he's not your son? What are you saying? Are you stupid or quite mad? Did you or did you not give birth to him?"

The old woman bent her head before that out-burst, half-closed her bleeding eyelids and re-plied:—

"Yes, Sir, I am stupid, perhaps. Mad—no! Would to God that I were mad! Then I should no longer suffer so. . . . But there are some things that your Honour cannot know, being still only a lad. I have white hair, I have suffered for a long time, I have seen many things, many things. . . . I have seen things, my dear young Sir, of which your Honour can have no conception."

"What have you seen, exactly? Speak!"—the doctor urged her.

"Terrible things! Horrible things!" the old woman lamented, shaking her head. "In those days your Honour was not born or thought of. I saw them with my own eyes—my eyes which since then have shed tears of blood. . . . Has your Honour heard speak of a certain Canebardo?"*

"Garibaldi?" asked the doctor, taken aback.

"Yes, Sir. Canebardo. He came to our parts and made the towns and country-side rebel against

* Sicilian corruption of the name Garibaldi.

every law of God and man. Have you heard speak
of him?"

"Yes, yes, go on! What has Garibaldi got to do
with it?"

"He has got to do with it because your Honour
should know that when he came here—that Canebardo—he gave orders to open all the prisons in all
the towns. Well, your Honour can imagine what
hellish furies were then let loose in our country
—the worst robbers, the worst assassins, bloody
wild beasts, maddened by many years of prison!
Amongst them there was one called Cola Camizzi
—he was the fiercest of them—a brigand chief
who killed his victims as if they were flies, just for
amusement, to test his powder, as he said—to see
if his gun was properly loaded. He settled down
in the open country, came in our direction and
passed through Farnia with a band of followers he
had collected among the peasants. He wasn't
satisfied with their number, but wanted more and
he killed all those who refused to join him. I had
then been married a few years, your Honour, and
already had those two sons who are over there, in
America—my darlings. We were living in the
farm of Pozzetto, which my husband—peace be
on his soul—had rented. Cola Camizzi passed by
and carried him off, too—he took my husband off
by force. . . . Two days later, I saw him come
back, looking like a corpse—he did not seem the

same man. He could not speak, his eyes were full
of the horrors he had seen, and he hid his hands—
poor fellow—from loathing of what he'd been
compelled to do with them. . . . Ah! my dear
young Sir, my heart was pierced by terror when I
saw him looking like that. 'My boy!' I called out
to him—(peace be on his soul)—'My boy, what
have you done?' He could not speak. 'Have you
run away from them, my boy? If they catch you,
what will happen? They will kill you!' My heart—
my heart told me what would happen. . . . He
stayed there for some time, sitting silent, close to
the hearth, looking at the floor, his hands always
hidden like this—under his jacket—and his eyes
like those of a madman. Then he said: 'Better
dead.' That was all he spoke. He stayed hidden for
three days; on the fourth he went out—we were
poor and had to work. He went out to work in the
fields. The evening came—he did not return. I
waited. Oh God! how I waited—But I knew
already, I had already pictured it all to myself. . . .
However, I thought, 'Who can say? Perhaps they
have not killed him—perhaps they have only taken
him away again.' Six days later I came to know that
Cola Camizzi and his band were in the Montelusa
Manor, the property of the Liguorian monks who
had run away. I walked there, almost out of my
mind. It was a day of terrible wind, young Sir,
such as I have never seen in my life. Have you

31

ever *seen* the wind? Well, that day, you could really see it! It seemed as if all the souls of the murdered ones were calling on men and on God for vengeance! I started in that hurricane and was carried along by it, almost torn to bits, and my screams were louder than its roar. I flew. I took scarcely an hour to reach the monastery, very high up, in a grove of black poplars.

"It had a large court/yard surrounded by a wall. The entrance was through a little door on one side, half hidden—I still remember—by a large clump of caper bushes which had their roots in the wall. I took a stone so as to knock louder. I knocked and knocked, but they would not open. I went on knocking, until at last they did open. Ah! God, what did I see then!——"

Maragrazia stood up, her face distorted by horror, her bleeding eyes staring wide. She stretched out one hand, her fingers cramped like claws. Her voice failed her, she could not go on.

"In the hands . . ." she said at last, "in the hands . . . of those assassins . . . in their hands. . . ."

She stopped again, almost choked, and moved her hand making the gesture of throwing some/thing.

"Well?" asked the doctor with a shiver.

"They were playing . . . there, in that court/yard . . . at bowls . . . playing with men's heads . . . black and covered with earth . . . they grasped

32

them by the hair . . . and . . . and one of the heads was my husband's . . . Cola Camizzi himself was holding it . . . he showed it to me. I uttered a scream which tore my throat and chest, a scream so loud that the murderers themselves shuddered at it. Cola Camizzi seized me by the neck to make me stop, but one of his men rushed at him furiously and then four or five or, maybe, ten others took courage from the first one's example and joined in, attacking him from every side. They too had had enough of the savage tyranny of that monster and revolted against him, Doctor, and I had the satis/ faction of seeing his throat cut there, under my very eyes, by his own companions—that dog of an assassin!"

The old woman sank into her chair, panting and exhausted, a prey to a convulsive fit of trembling.

The young doctor watched her with a look of mingled pity, disgust and horror. When his feeling of nausea had passed and he was able to think calmly again, he still failed to understand what connection that ghastly story could have with the case of the other son. He asked her to explain.

"Wait!" replied the old woman, as soon as she regained her breath. "The one who came to my defence and started the revolt was called Marco Trupia."

"Ah!" exclaimed the doctor. "So that Rocco . . ."

"His son," replied Maragrazia. "But think, Doctor, think! Could I have become the wife of that man after what I'd been through? He insisted on taking me; for three months he kept me with him, he tied me up and gagged me, because I screamed and bit. . . . After three months the authorities got hold of him and shut him up in prison, where he died soon after. But I was left pregnant.

"Ah! young Sir, I swear to you that I wanted to tear out my inside—it seemed to me that I was doomed to give birth to a monster! I felt that I could never even touch the child. At the thought that I might have to suckle him, I screamed like a madwoman. I nearly died when he was born. My mother (peace be on her soul!) looked after me and did not even let me see the baby, but took him straight off to the father's family, where he was brought up. . . . Now, do not you think, Doctor, that I can rightly say that he is not my son?"

Absorbed in thought, the young doctor did not answer for a moment; then he said:—

"But he—after all—your son, what fault is it of his?"

"None!" replied the old woman, "and never, never have my lips uttered a word against him. Never, Doctor, quite the contrary, I assure you. But what can I do if I cannot bear the sight of him, even at a distance? He is the living image of his

father, my dear young Sir, in features, in build and
even in his voice. I begin to tremble, as soon as I
see him, and I get into a cold sweat! I'm no longer
myself; my blood revolts, you see. What can I
do?"

She stopped a moment, wiping her eyes with
the back of her hand; then, fearing that the party
of emigrants would leave Farnia without the letter
for her real sons—her adored sons—she plucked
up courage and roused the doctor from his abstraction, saying:—

"If your Honour would do me the favour you
promised. . . ."

With an effort the young man shook off his
thoughts, moved his chair up to the desk, and told
her that he was ready. Then once again she began
to dictate in the same whining tone:—

"*Dear sons . . .*"

BETTER THINK TWICE ABOUT IT

BETTER THINK TWICE ABOUT IT

FOR the past three days, the home of Professor Agostino Toti had lacked the tranquility and gaiety which he had come to look upon as his right.

One could hardly describe the professor as a fine figure of a man for his age. He was about seventy, very small, save for his large bald head, had no neck, and a body quite out of proportion to his two bird-like sticks of legs. Professor Toti had not the faintest illusions about his personal appearance, nor did he for one moment imagine that his pretty little wife, Maddalena, who was not yet twenty-seven, could love him for himself alone.

It is true that he had chosen to marry a poor girl to whom he was able to offer a rise in station. She was only the daughter of a door-keeper at the High School and had become the wife of a Professor of Natural Science, on the permanent staff, who in a few months' time was due to qualify for the full pension. Not only that, but he was a rich man besides, thanks to an unexpected legacy which had come to him two years previously—a windfall of some two·hundred·thousand lire, fallen like manna from heaven after the death of his brother, who had left for Roumania many years before and had never married.

Professor Toti did not, however, consider that all this entitled him to expect cheerfulness and tranquility in his home; being a philosopher, he knew that a pretty young wife needed something more.

Had he come into his fortune before he married, he might perhaps have had the right to ask his little Maddalena to be patient for a while, as it would not be long before his death would enable her to make up for the sacrifice of having married an old man. But alas! those two·hundred·thousand lire had arrived too late—a couple of years after his marriage—by which time Professor Toti had already . . . had already had the philosophy to realise that the trifling pension which he would one day leave his wife was not an adequate compen· sation for the sacrifice she had made in marrying him.

Having therefore made every concession at an earlier date, Professor Toti considered that he had a better right than ever to expect peace and gaiety in his house now that there was that valuable legacy in addition. All the more so since, as a truly wise and kind·hearted man, he had not rested content with being a benefactor to his wife, but had also been willing to be one to . . . well yes, to *him* too, to his good Giacomino, who had been one of his most promising pupils at the High School, a well-conducted young fellow, rather shy, but with very nice manners, handsome and with the fair curly hair that one sees in pictures of angels.

Yes indeed, old Professor Agostino Toti had thought of everything. Giacomino Delisi was out of work, he was in a state of deep depression and was losing heart; so he—Professor Toti—had found the young man a post in the Bank of Agriculture where he had invested the two-hundred-thousand lire of inheritance.

There was also a baby now in the household—a little darling, two-and-a-half years old—to whom the professor was utterly devoted, a loving slave. The daily lectures at the High School seemed interminable as he waited for the hour when he could hurry home and satisfy all the whims and fancies of his little tyrant. He could indeed have sent in his resignation when he received his legacy and have retired without waiting for the maximum pension; in this way he would have been free to devote all his time to the baby. But he would not hear of such a thing. True, he had always found his professorship a great worry, but since he had taken it on, he would go through with it to the

41

bitter end. It would be a sin to let slip the right to
the full pension. Why, it was for that very reason
that he had married—in order that some one
might secure a benefit out of what had been a
lifelong trial to himself.

Having married with that single aim—to act as
benefactor to a poor young girl—his love for his
wife was only of a semi/fatherly nature. His feel/
ings towards her became still more paternal after
her baby's birth and he would almost have pre/
ferred the child to call him 'Grandad' rather than
'Daddy'. It hurt him to hear that false statement
uttered all unknowingly by the lips of the innocent
baby. He seemed to see in it some insult to his
love for the child. But he was helpless in the
matter: he had to give Nini a kiss when the child
called him 'Daddy', though the use of the name
made people smile in no kindly way. How could
those evil/minded persons understand the tender
love he felt for the little one, or his happiness at the
benefits he had conferred and was still conferring
on a woman and also on a fine young fellow and on
the baby, and lastly on himself too—yes, indeed—
on himself, since he was thus able to enjoy the
remaining years of his life by spending them in
cheerful, loving society and to have a little angel
as his close companion during the last stage of his
journey to the grave.

Let them laugh to their hearts' content, those

malicious onlookers. . . . It's easy to laugh in that
foolish fashion. Why didn't they put themselves in
his place and they would understand. They could
only see the comic—the more than comic—the
grotesque aspect of the case, because they could
not enter into his feelings. Well, what did it
matter to him, since he was happy. . . .

Unfortunately, however, for the past three
days . . .

What could have happened? His Maddalena's
eyes were swollen and red from weeping; she com;
plained of a severe headache and would not leave
her room.

"Ah! Youth! . . . youth! . . ." sighed Pro;
fessor Toti, shaking his head with a knowing look
in his eyes, as he smiled sadly. "Some cloud or
other . . . a passing storm . . ."

With Nini as companion he wandered round the
house, restless, anxious and also rather cross, be;
cause—after all—really he didn't deserve to be
treated like that by his wife and Giacomino.
Young people don't have to count the days—they
have so many more still before them; but to a
poor old man the loss of a single day is a serious
blow; and by now it was already three days since
his wife had left him like this, feeling quite lost in
his own home, like a fly that has had its head taken
off. It was three days now since he had heard her
sweet voice singing the little airs and ballads which

she knew how to sing so prettily—three days since she had lavished on him any of the little attentions to which he had become so accustomed.

Nini too was very solemn, as if he understood that Mummy was not in the mood to take any interest in him. The professor took him from one room to another—he was so very short himself that he hardly needed to stoop at all, as he led the child by the hand. He lifted him up to the piano, played a few notes, then abandoned the instrument with a yawn and an impatient little sniff; sat down and took Nini on his knees to play 'Ride-a-cock-horse' with him and stood up again, feeling utterly miserable. Five or six times he had tried to induce his little wife to speak of her trouble.

"Feeling bad, are you? . . . Are you feeling very bad?"

But Maddalenina still failed to tell him anything. She wept, begged him to close the balcony shutters and take Nini away—she wished to be left alone, to lie in the dark.

"Is your head aching?"

Poor girl, she had such a bad headache. . . . Evidently the quarrel had been a very serious one indeed.

Professor Toti went to the kitchen and tried to approach the servant, to obtain some information from her. He could not speak at all plainly to her, for he knew that the maid was by no means a friend

44

of his: outside the house she let her tongue wag freely, making coarse fun of him, just as every one else did—the silly fool who ought to have known better.

Failing to discover anything from his talk with the maid, Professor Toti adopted a heroic resolution. He took Nini to 'Mummy' and asked her to dress the child up in his best clothes.

"Why?" asked Maddalena.

"I'm taking him out for a little turn," he answered. "It's a holiday today . . . the poor child's getting very bored shut up in the house."

'Mummy' did not like the idea. She knew the unkind way in which people laughed at the sight of the old professor going hand in hand with the small child; she knew that at times they had even gone so far as to say, with shameless irony—"Your son does take after you, Professor. He's so like you . . ."

Professor Toti, however, insisted.

"Just a little turn—to amuse ourselves."

He then took the child to the house of Giacomino Delisi.

The young man lived with a sister a few years older than himself, who had mothered him in his early days. At first the Signorina Agata had been full of gratitude to Professor Toti for his kindness to her brother. At that time she was in complete ignorance as to the reasons for his conduct. She was an extremely religious woman and accordingly, when she came to learn the truth of the case, she regarded the professor as a fiend in human shape, in that he had tempted her Giacomino and led him into mortal sin.

After ringing at the door, Professor Toti had to wait outside, with the child, for a considerable time. The Signorina Agata had come and peeped through the judas-hole and hurried away. No doubt she had gone to inform her brother that he had called—she would shortly return to tell him that Giacomino was not at home.

At last she appeared—a frosty, sour-faced woman, dressed all in black, with waxy complexion and livid circles round her eyes. The moment she opened the door, she assailed him, all quivering with emotion:—

"I beg your pardon! . . . What does this mean? . . . You even go so far as to look him up in his house, now? . . . And what's this I see. . . . You've brought the baby? . . . You've brought the child here too! . . ."

Professor Toti had not expected an attack of this nature. Completely taken aback, he looked first at the Signorina, then at the child, and smiled and stammered.

"Why . . . why? . . . What is it? . . . Can't I . . . can't I come to . . . ?"

BETTER THINK TWICE ABOUT IT

"He's not at home," she hastened to answer in a dry, unsympathetic tone. "Giacomino's not at home."

"Very well," said Professor Toti, with a little bow. "But you, Signorina—I hope you won't mind my saying so—you treat me in a way which . . . how shall I put it? . . . I have no recollection of ever behaving towards either your brother or yourself in a way that would justify . . ."

"That's exactly the point, Professor," interrupted Signorina Agata, who had been slightly mollified by his words. "Believe me, we are . . . yes, we are indeed most grateful to you. But surely you must understand that . . ."

Professor Toti smiled again, half closed his eyes, raised his hand and tapped his breast several times with his finger-tips to intimate to her that, when it came to understanding anything, she could leave the matter to him.

"I am an old man, Signorina," he said, "and I understand . . . I understand many things. Now here is one of the first of those things—when anyone is in a temper, one must let them cool down; and when misunderstandings arise, the best course is to clear them up . . . to clear them up, Signorina, in all frankness, without any subterfuge, without becoming heated over it. . . . Don't you agree?"

"Yes, indeed," replied Signorina Agata, admitting this general proposition.

"Very well then," resumed Professor Toti, "kindly let me come in, and you go and call Giacomino."

"But if he's not at home?"

"Come, come! You mustn't tell me that he's not at home. Giacomino is in this house and you ought to go and call him. Say that we shall clear matters up calmly . . . quite calmly. I am an old man and I understand all about it, because I was once young myself, Signorina. Quite calmly, tell him. Please let me come in."

Allowed at last to enter the humble parlour, Professor Toti sat down and took Nini between his legs. He resigned himself to the prospect of being kept waiting for a considerable time before Giacomino could be persuaded by his sister to appear.

"No, don't go over there, Nini . . . behave nicely . . . be a good boy," he said every now and then to the child, who wanted to wander off to a fancy table sparkling with cheap china ornaments. Meanwhile he racked his brains to discover how the devil such a grave incident could have taken place in his own house and he not have been aware of it. His Maddalena was such a good little girl. What could she possibly have done to have aroused such violent, determined resentment in this household, even in Giacomino's sister?

Up till then, the professor had supposed that there had been only a temporary estrange‹

ment, but he now began to grow quite seriously
worried.

At last Giacomino appeared. Good heavens!
how upset he looked, and what a cross face! And—
but no, no that would never do!—there he was
coldly pushing away the child who had run up,
holding out his little hands in greeting, with a cry
of "Giami! Giami!"

"Giacomino!" exclaimed Professor Toti in a
severe tone, wounded by such conduct.

"What is it you have to say to me, Professor?"
the young man hastened to enquire and, as he
spoke, he avoided looking the professor straight in
the face. "I'm not well . . . I was in bed. . . .
Really I'm not fit to talk or even to stand the sight
of anyone . . ."

"But the baby?"

"Here's a kiss for him," said Giacomino and
stooped down to kiss the child.

"So you're feeling ill?" resumed Professor Toti,
slightly pacified by that kiss. "I thought you must
be. That's why I've come. Your head bad, eh?
Sit down, sit down and let's talk. . . . Nini, did
you hear that? Giami has the *bua*. . . . Yes, he's
got the *bua* . . . poor Giami, so you must be very
good, Nini. We'll soon be going . . . I wanted
to ask you," he continued, turning to Giacomino,
"whether the Manager of the Bank of Agriculture
said anything to you."

49

"No, why?" replied Giacomino, still more upset at these words.

"Because I spoke to him about you yesterday," replied Professor Toti with a little smile of mystery. "Your salary is not very large, my son. And, you know, a little word from myself . . ."

Giacomino shifted uneasily on his chair and clenched his fists so tightly that his nails dug into the palms of his hands.

"I thank you for what you've done, Professor," he said, "but please note that I want you to do me the favour—the great favour—of not putting yourself out in future on my account."

"You really mean it?" answered Professor Toti, with that little smile still on his lips. "Bravo! So we've no longer need of anyone, eh? . . . But suppose I should want to help you for my own satisfaction—my own pleasure? My dear boy, if I am not to take an interest in you, whom d'you think I am going to take an interest in? . . . I'm an old man, Giacomino, and old men—mind, I'm not speaking of the selfish ones among us—old men who have worked as hard to make good, as I have done, enjoy seeing deserving young men like your‑self make progress in their careers, thanks to the help we can give them. The old find pleasure in the gaiety and hopefulness of the young, in seeing them gradually make their way in the world. And then, as regards yourself—surely you realise that

I always look upon you as my son? . . . Good heavens! What's the matter? . . . You're not crying?"

Giacomino had in fact hidden his face in his hands. From his convulsive movements it looked as if he were struggling to avoid breaking into a fit of tears.

Nini looked at him timidly, then turned to the professor and said:—

"Giami . . . *Bua.* . . ."

The professor rose and was about to put his hand on Giacomino's shoulder, when the young man sprang up as if in horror at the thought of such contact. His face distorted by a look of fierce determination, he shouted wildly:—

"Don't come near me, Professor. Go away—I implore you—go away. You're making me suffer the tortures of the damned. I don't deserve your affection and I don't want it . . . I don't want it, I tell you. . . . For goodness sake be off and take the child with you, and forget my very existence."

Professor Toti was dumbfounded.

"What do you mean?" he asked.

"I'll tell you straight out," replied Giacomino. "I'm engaged to be married, Professor. Do you understand? I'm engaged."

Professor Toti tottered as if he had been clubbed on the head. He threw up his hands stammering:—

51

"You? . . . en . . . en . . . engaged?"

"Yes, Sir. And so you see all is finished . . . it's finished for good. . . . Now you'll under= stand that I can no longer see you . . . see you here . . ."

"You're turning me out?" asked Professor Toti in a voice that was barely audible.

"No," Giacomino hastened to reply, in a tone of grief. "But it is better that you . . . that you should go, Professor . . ."

Go! The professor sank upon his chair. He felt his legs suddenly giving way beneath him. He put his head between his hands and groaned.

"My God! What a disaster. . . . So that's the explanation. . . . Oh what am I to do—what am I to do. . . . But when did this happen? How? Not a word of it to me! Whom are you engaged to?"

"It happened here . . . a short time ago," said Giacomino. "She's like me—an orphan, and poor —and she's a friend of my sister."

Professor Toti looked at him stupefied. His mouth was open, his eyes dull; for several seconds he could not utter a word, then he faltered:—

"And . . . and . . . and so everything is drop= ped, like that . . . and . . . and no further thought is given to . . . to anyone . . . no further account taken of anything. . . ."

Giacomino felt the charge of ingratitude which

underlay these words; in a gloomy spirit of rebellion he retorted:—

"I beg your pardon, but were you expecting me to become a slave?"

"*I* expect *you* to become a slave?" exclaimed Professor Toti in rising tones. "*I?* You can ask that of *me*, when I have made you the master of my house? Ah! that . . . that really is the basest of ingratitude. What advantage d'you think I have gained? What have I got out of it, except the mockery of those fools who can't enter into my feelings? So *you* don't understand either—you've never understood my feelings? I'm only a poor old man approaching very near the end of my life, but I have been able to derive a tranquil satisfaction from the thought of leaving behind me a happy little family, which was well provided for and had made a good start in life! I am seventy years old, Giacomino, and soon—in a few days perhaps—I shall have left you. What has made you go out of your senses, my son? I am bequeathing my whole estate to the three of you. . . . What more do you want? . . . I don't know yet, I don't want to know who your fiancée is. Since it is you who have chosen her, she's sure to be a decent girl, because you're a fine young fellow. But, consider a moment—consider . . . it isn't possible that you could have found a better girl, Giacomino, when everything is taken into consideration . . . I'm not speaking only of the fact that you would be left in comfort-able circumstances, quite well off, in fact; but here you've already got your own little family, with myself only as an extra person in it—I don't count, and anyhow I'm only here for a short time. . . . In what way does my presence worry you? I'm like your father, so to speak . . . I could even, if you wished and if it would make you any happier. . . . But tell me, tell me how it came about? What happened? How did your head come to be turned, all of a sudden, like this? Explain to me, my boy. Tell me all about it. . . ."

Professor Toti went up and was about to put his hand on Giacomino's shoulder, but the young man shrank back, almost with a shudder, and avoided his touch.

"But, Professor," he cried. "Can't you under-stand? Can't you see that all this kindness of yours . . ."

"Well?"

"Oh! leave me alone. Don't force me to speak out. . . . Oh! my God. How is it that you can't understand that certain things can only be done on the quiet, that it's no longer possible to go on doing them when *you* know all about it, and every-body makes a joke of it?"

"Everybody? I don't care *that* for them," cried the professor. "So you see . . ."

"Oh! do leave me alone," repeated Giacomino,

waving his arms wildly, in a frenzy of excitement. "Look, Professor. Look! There are so many other young men in need of help."

These last words wounded Toti deeply: he regarded them as an atrocious and quite uncalled-for insult to his wife. He turned pale; then, with a quiver of rage which brought the blood to his cheeks again, he replied:—

"Maddalenina is a young girl, but thank God she is modest and virtuous, as you well know. Maddalenina may die of this blow, because it has stabbed her to the heart . . . how else d'you think she would take it? It is *there*, in the heart that you have stabbed her, ungrateful fellow that you are. And now, in addition, you're insulting her. Aren't you ashamed of yourself? Can you stand there before me and feel no remorse? You can actually say that to my face, Giacomino? D'you think that she can change over from one person to another, as if it were a trifle? You can say that to the mother of this baby? What can you be thinking of? How dare you speak in that way!"

Giacomino was so surprised that he found it difficult to answer.

"I?" he said. "But . . . but . . . that question ought to be put to you, Professor. Excuse my saying so, but how can *you* speak in that way? You're not talking seriously?"

Professor Toti threw up his hands and pressed

them to his mouth, blinked, shook his head violently to and fro and burst into a flood of tears. At this point, Nini also started crying. The professor heard him, hurried over to him and embraced him, murmuring:—

"Oh! my poor Nini . . . what a terrible blow . . . ruin, complete ruin, poor little Nini. . . . What will become of your poor Mummy now? And what will happen to you, my Nini, with a little mother like yours, so inexperienced and with no one to guide her? . . . Oh! God, what a scoundrel!"

He raised his head and peered at Giacomino through his tears, saying:—

"I am weeping because I blame myself so bitterly: I took you up, made you at home in my house and always spoke to her so highly of you— I . . . I removed all the scruples she felt about falling in love with you . . . and . . . and, now that she has come to love you truly . . . now that she is the mother of this darling child . . . you . . . you . . ."

He broke off; then, with a sudden savage resolution, he added excitedly:—

"Have a care, Giacomino! You have a care! I am quite capable of presenting myself at your fiancée's house, accompanied by this child."

Giacomino had been in a cold sweat, though he felt at the same time as if he were on hot coals

when he heard the professor's reproaches and witnessed his distress. At this concluding threat, he
stepped forward and held up his clasped hands
with an imploring gesture.

"Professor, Professor," he begged him. "You
don't want to make a spectacle of yourself—you
don't want to cover yourself with ridicule."

"With ridicule?" shouted the old man. "What
d'you think I care about ridicule, when I see the
impending ruin of a poor woman, of yourself and
of this little innocent one. . . . Come along, Nini,
let's be off . . . we must go."

Giacomino stepped in front of him.

"Professor, you can't really do that?"

"I most certainly can and will," cried the professor with a look of great determination. "And—
what's more—to prevent you from marrying, I am
also capable of having you turned out of the Bank.
. . . I give you three days' time."

Holding the child's hand he turned round at the
door-way and added:

"You'd better think twice about it, Giacomino!"

THE JAR

THE JAR

THE olive crop was a bumper one that year: the trees had flowered luxuriantly the year before, and, though there had been a long spell of misty weather at the time, the fruit had set well. Lollo Zirafa had a fine plantation on his farm at Primosole. Reckoning that the five old jars of glazed earthenware which he had in his wine-cellar would not suffice to hold all the oil of that harvest, he had placed an order well beforehand at Santo Stefano Di Camastra, where they are made. His new jar was to be of greater capacity—breast-high and pot-bellied; it would be the mother-superior to the little community of five other jars.

I need scarcely say that Don Lollo Zirafa had had a dispute with the potter concerning this jar. It would indeed be hard to name anyone with whom he had not picked a quarrel: for every trifle—be it merely a stone that had fallen from his boundary wall, or a handful of straw—he would shout out to the servants to saddle his mule, so that he could hurry to the town and file a suit. He had half-ruined himself, because of the large sums he had

had to spend on court fees and lawyers' bills, bringing actions against one person after another, which always ended in his having to pay the costs of both sides. People said that his legal adviser grew so tired of seeing him appear two or three times a week that he tried to reduce the frequency of his visits by making him a present of a volume which looked like a prayer-book: it contained the judicial code—the idea being that he should take the trouble to see for himself what the rights and wrongs of the case were before hurrying to bring a suit.

Previously, when anyone had a difference with him, they would try to make him lose his temper by shouting out: "Saddle the mule!" but now they changed it to "Go and look up your pocket-code!" Don Lollo would reply: "That I will and I'll break the lot of you, you sons of bitches!"

In course of time, the new jar, for which he had paid the goodly sum of four florins, duly arrived; until room could be found for it in the wine-cellar, it was lodged in the crushing-shed for a few days. Never had there been a finer jar. It was quite distressing to see it lodged in that foul den, which reeked of stale grape-juice and had that musty smell of places deprived of light and air.

It was now two days since the harvesting of the olives had begun, and Don Lollo was almost beside himself, having to supervise not only the men who were beating down the fruit from the trees, but also a number of others who had come with mule<loads of manure to be deposited in heaps on the hill<side, where he had a field in which he was going to sow beans for the next crop. He felt that it was really more than one man could manage, he was at his wits' ends whom to attend to: cursing like a trooper, he vowed he would exterminate, first this man and then that, if an olive—one single olive—was miss< ing: he almost talked as if he had counted them, one by one, on his trees; then he would turn to the muleteers and utter the direst threats as to what would happen, if any one heap of manure were not exactly the same size as the others. A little white cap on his head, his sleeves rolled up and his shirt open at the front, he rushed here, there and everywhere; his face was a bright red and poured with sweat, his eyes glared about him wolfishly, while his hands rubbed angrily at his shaven chin, where a fresh growth of beard always sprouted the moment the razor had left it.

At the close of the third day's work, three of the farm<hands—rough fellows with dirty, brutish faces —went to the crushing<shed; they had been beating the olive trees and went to replace their ladders and poles in the shed. They stood aghast at the sight of the fine new jar in two pieces, looking for all the world as if some one had caught hold of the bulging front and cut it off with a sharp sweep of the knife.

"Oh, my God! look! look!"

"How on earth has that happened?"

"My holy aunt! When Don Lollo hears of it!
The new jar! What a pity, though!"

The first of the three, more frightened than his
companions, proposed to shut the door again at
once and to sneak away very quietly, leaving their
ladders and poles outside leaning up against the
wall; but the second took him up sharply.

"That's a stupid idea! You can't try that on
Don Lollo. As like as not he'd believe we broke
it ourselves. No, we all stay here!"

He went out of the shed and, using his hands as
a trumpet, called out:—

"Don Lollo! Oh! Don LOLLOOOOO!"

When the farmer came up and saw the damage,
he fell into a towering passion. First he vented his
fury on the three men. He seized one of them by
the throat, pinned him against the wall, and
shouted:—

"By the Virgin's blood, you'll pay for that!"

The other two sprang forward in wild excite,
ment, fell upon Don Lollo and pulled him away.
Then his mad rage turned against himself: he
stamped his feet, flung his cap on the ground, and
slapped his cheeks, bewailing his loss with screams
suited only for the death of a relation.

"The new jar! A four,florin jar! Brand new!"

Who could have broken it? Could it possibly

have broken of itself? Certainly some one must have broken it, out of malice or from envy at his possession of such a beauty. But when? How? There was no sign of violence. Could it conceivably have come in a broken condition from the pottery? No, it rang like a bell on its arrival.

As soon as the farm-hands saw that their master's first outburst of rage was spent, they began to console him, saying that he should not take it so to heart, as the jar could be mended. After all, the break was not a bad one, for the front had come away all in one piece; a clever rivetter could repair it and make it as good as new. Zi' Dima Licasi* was just the man for the job: he had invented a marvellous cement made of some composition which he kept a strict secret—miraculous stuff! Once it had set, you couldn't loosen it, even with a hammer. So they suggested that, if Don Lollo agreed, Zi' Dima Licasi should turn up at daybreak and—as sure as eggs were eggs—the jar would be repaired and be even better than a new one.

For a long time Don Lollo turned a deaf ear to their advice—it was quite useless, there was no making good the damage—but in the end he allowed himself to be persuaded and punctually at daybreak Zi' Dima Licasi arrived at Primosole, with his outfit in a basket slung on his back. He turned

*Zio (uncle) is used as a familiar prefix.

out to be a misshapen old man with swollen, crooked joints, like the stem of an ancient Saracen olive tree. To extract a word from him, it looked as if you would have to use a pair of forceps on his mouth. His ungraceful figure seemed to radiate discontent or gloom, due perhaps to his disappoint‹ ment that no one had so far been found willing to do justice to his merits as an inventor. For Zi' Dima Licasi had not yet patented his discovery; he wanted to make a name for it first by its success‹ ful application. Meanwhile he felt it necessary to keep a sharp look‹out, for fear lest some one steal the secret of his process.

"Let me see that cement of yours," began Don Lollo in a distrustful tone, after examining him from head to foot for several minutes.

Zi' Dima declined, with a dignified shake of the head.

"You'll see its results."

"But, will it hold?"

Zi' Dima put his basket on the ground and took out from it a red bundle composed of a large cotton handkerchief, much the worse for wear, wrapped round and round something. He began to unroll it very carefully, while they all stood round watch‹ ing him with close attention. When at last, how‹ ever, nothing came to light save a pair of spectacles with bridge and sides broken and tied up with string, there was a general laugh. Zi' Dima took no notice, but wiped his fingers before handling the spectacles, then put them on and, with much solemnity, began his examination of the jar, which had been brought outside on to the threshing, floor. Finally he said:

"It'll hold."

"But I can't trust cement alone," Don Lollo stipulated, "I must have rivets as well."

"I'm off," Zi' Dima promptly replied, standing up and replacing his basket on his back.

Don Lollo caught hold of his arm:—

"Off? Where to? You've got no more manners than a pig! . . . Just look at this pauper putting on an air of royalty! . . . Why! you wretched fool, I've got to put oil in that jar, and don't you know that oil oozes? Yards and yards to join together, and you talk of using cement alone! I want rivets— cement and rivets. It's for me to decide."

Zi' Dima shut his eyes, closed his lips tightly and shook his head. People were all like that—they refused to give him the satisfaction of turning out a neat bit of work, performed with artistic thorough, ness and proving the wonderful virtues of his cement.

"If," he said, "the jar doesn't ring as true as a bell once more . . ."

"I won't listen to a word," Don Lollo broke in. "I want rivets! I'll pay you for cement and rivets. How much will it come to?"

BETTER THINK TWICE ABOUT IT

"If I use cement only . . ."

"My God! what an obstinate fellow! What did I say? I told you I wanted rivets. We'll settle the terms after the work is done. I've no more time to waste on you."

And he went off to look after his men.

In a state of great indignation Zi' Dima started on the job and his temper continued to rise as he bored hole after hole in the jar and in its broken section—holes for his iron rivets. Along with the squeaking of his tool went a running accompaniment of grunts which grew steadily louder and more frequent; his fury made his eyes more piercing and bloodshot and his face became green with bile. When he had finished that first operation, he flung his borer angrily into the basket and held the detached portion up against the jar to satisfy himself that the holes were at equal distances and fitted one another; next he took his pliers and cut a length of iron wire into as many pieces as he needed rivets, and then called to one of the men who were beating the olive trees to come and help him.

"Cheer up, Zi' Dima!" said the labourer, seeing how upset the old man looked.

Zi' Dima raised his hand with a savage gesture. He opened the tin which contained the cement and held it up towards heaven, as if offering it to God, seeing that men refused to recognise its value. Then he began to spread it with his finger all round the detached portion and along the broken edge of the jar. Taking his pliers and the iron rivets he had prepared, he crept inside the open belly of the jar and instructed the farm/hand to hold the piece up, fitting it closely to the jar as he had himself done a short time previously. Before starting to put in the rivets, he spoke from inside the jar:—

"Pull! Pull! Tug at it with all your might! . . . You see it doesn't come loose. Curses on people who won't believe me! Knock it! Yes, knock it! . . . Doesn't it ring like a bell, even with me inside it? Go and tell your master that!"

"It's for the top/dog to give orders, Zi' Dima," said the man with a sigh, "and it's for the under/dog to carry them out. Put the rivets in. Put 'em in."

Zi' Dima began to pass the bits of iron through the adjacent holes, one on each side of the crack, twisting up the ends with his pliers. It took him an hour to put them all in, and he poured with sweat inside the jar. As he worked, he complained of his misfortune and the farm/hand stayed near, trying to console him.

"Now help me to get out," said Zi' Dima, when all was finished.

But large though its belly was, the jar had a distinctly narrow neck—a fact which Zi' Dima had overlooked, being so absorbed in his grievance.

Now, try as he would, he could not manage to squeeze his way out. Instead of helping him, the farm-hand stood idly by, convulsed with laughter. So there was poor Zi' Dima, imprisoned in the jar which he had mended and—there was no use in blinking at the fact—in a jar which would have to be broken to let him out, and this time broken for good.

Hearing the laughter and shouts, Don Lollo came rushing up. Inside the jar Zi' Dima was spitting like an angry cat.

"Let me out," he screamed, "for God's sake! I want to get out! Be quick! Help!"

Don Lollo was quite taken aback and unable to believe his own ears.

"What? Inside there? He's rivetted himself up inside?"

Then he went up to the jar and shouted out to Zi' Dima:—

"Help you? What help do you think I can give you? You stupid old dodderer, what d'you mean by it? Why couldn't you measure it first? Come, have a try! Put an arm out . . . that's it! Now the head! Up you come! . . . No, no, gently! . . . Down again. . . . Wait a bit! . . . Not that way. . . . Down, get down. . . . How on earth could you do such a thing? . . . What about my jar now? . . .

"Keep calm! Keep calm!" he recommended to

all the onlookers, as if it was they who were becom‚
ing excited and not himself. . . . "My head's
going round! Keep calm! This is quite a new
point! Get me my mule!"

He rapped the jar with his knuckles. Yes, it
really rang like a bell once again.

"Fine! Repaired as good as new. . . . You wait
a bit!" he said to the prisoner; then instructed his
man to be off and saddle the mule. He rubbed his
forehead vigorously with his fingers, and con‚
tinued:—

"I wonder what's the best course. That's not a
jar, it's a contrivance of the devil himself. . . .
Keep still! Keep still!" he exclaimed, rushing up to
steady the jar, in which Zi' Dima, now in a tower‚
ing passion, was struggling like a wild animal in a
trap.

"It's a new point, my good man, which the
lawyer must settle. I can't rely on my own judg‚
ment. . . . Where's that mule? Hurry up with
the mule! . . . I'll go straight there and back.
You must wait patiently: it's in your own interest.
. . . Meanwhile, keep quiet, be calm! I must look
after my own rights. And, first of all, to put myself
in the right, I fulfil my obligation. Here you are!
I am paying you for your work, for a whole day's
work. Here are your five lire. Is that enough?"

"I don't want anything," shouted Zi' Dima. "I
want to get out!"

BETTER THINK TWICE ABOUT IT

"You shall get out, but meanwhile I, for my part, am paying you. There they are—five lire."

He took the money out of his waistcoat pocket and tossed it into the jar, then enquired in a tone of great concern:—

"Have you had any lunch? . . . Bread and something to eat with it, at once! . . . What! You don't want it? Well, then, throw it to the dogs! I shall have done my duty when I've given it to you."

Having ordered the food, he mounted and set out for the town. His wild gesticulations made those who saw him galloping past think that he might well be hastening to shut himself up in a lunatic asylum.

As luck would have it, he did not have to spend much time in the ante-room before being admitted to the lawyer's study; he had, however, to wait a long while before the lawyer could finish laughing, after the matter had been related to him. Annoyed at the amusement he caused, Don Lollo said irritably:—

"Excuse me, but I don't see anything to laugh at. It's all very well for your Honour, who is not the sufferer, but the jar is my property."

The lawyer, however, continued to laugh and then made him tell the story all over again, just as it had happened, so that he could raise another laugh out of it.

"Inside, eh? So he'd rivetted himself inside?"
And what did Don Lollo want to do? . . . "To
ke . . . to ke . . . keep him there inside—ha! ha!
ha! . . . keep him there inside, so as not to lose
the jar?"

"Why should I lose it?" cried Don Lollo, clench‹
ing his fists. "Why should I put up with the loss of
my money, and have people laughing at me?"

"But don't you know what that's called?" said
the lawyer at last. "It's called 'wrongful confine‹
ment'."

"Confinement? Well, who's confined him? He's
confined himself! What fault is that of mine?"

The lawyer then explained to him that the
matter gave rise to two cases: on the one hand he,
Don Lollo, must straightway liberate the prisoner,
if he wished to escape from being prosecuted for
wrongful confinement; while, on the other hand,
the rivetter would be responsible for making good
the loss resulting from his lack of skill or his
stupidity.

"Ah!" said Don Lollo, with a sigh of relief.
"So he'll have to pay me for my jar?"

"Wait a bit," remarked the lawyer. "Not as if
it were a new jar, remember!"

"Why not?"

"Because it was a broken one, badly broken,
too."

"Broken! No, Sir. Not broken. It's perfectly

sound now and better than ever it was—he says so himself. And if I have to break it again, I shall not be able to have it mended. The jar will be ruined, Sir!"

The lawyer assured him that that point would be taken into account and that the rivetter would have to pay the value which the jar had in its present condition.

"Therefore," he counselled, "get the man him⁄self to give you an estimate of its value first."

"I kiss your hands," Don Lollo murmured, and hurried away.

On his return home towards evening, he found all his labourers engaged in a celebration around the inhabited jar. The watch⁄dogs joined in the festivities with joyous barks and capers. Zi' Dima had not only calmed down, but had even come to enjoy his curious adventure and was able to laugh at it, with the melancholy humour of the unfor⁄tunate.

Don Lollo drove them all aside and bent down to look into the jar.

"Hallo! Getting along well?"

"Splendid! An open⁄air life for me!" replied the man. "It's better than in my own house."

"I'm glad to hear it. Meanwhile I'd just like you to know that that jar cost me four florins when it was new. How much do you think it is worth now?"

THE JAR

"With me inside it?" asked Zi' Dima.

The rustics laughed.

"Silence!" shouted Don Lollo. "Either your cement is of some use or it is of no use. There is no third possibility. If it is of no use, you are a fraud. If it is of some use, the jar, in its present condition, must have a value. What is that value? I ask for your estimate."

After a space for reflection, Zi' Dima said:—

"Here is my answer: if you had let me mend it with cement only—as I wanted to do—first of all I should not have been. shut up inside it and the jar would have had its original value, without any doubt. But spoilt by these rivets, which had to be done from inside, it has lost most of its value. It's worth a third of its former price, more or less."

"One third? That's one florin, thirty three cents."

"Maybe less, but not more than that."

"Well," said Don Lollo. "Promise me that you'll pay me one florin thirty three cents."

"What?" asked Zi' Dima, as if he did not grasp the point.

"I will break the jar to let you out," replied Don Lollo. "And—the lawyer tells me—you are to pay me its value according to your own estimate—one florin thirty three."

"I? Pay?" laughed Zi' Dima, "I'd sooner stay here till I rot!"

75

With some difficulty he managed to extract from his pocket a short and peculiarly foul pipe and lighted it, puffing out the smoke through the neck of the jar.

Don Lollo stood there scowling: the possibility that Zi' Dima would no longer be willing to leave the jar, had not been foreseen either by himself or by the lawyer. What step should he take now? He was on the point of ordering them to saddle the mule, but reflected that it was already evening.

"Oh ho!" he said. "So you want to take up your abode in my jar! I call upon all you men as witnesses to his statement. He refuses to come out, in order to escape from paying. I am quite prepared to break it. Well, as you insist on staying there, I shall take proceedings against you tomorrow for unlawful occupancy of the jar and for preventing me from my rightful use of it."

Zi' Dima blew out another puff of smoke and answered calmly:—

"No, your Honour. I don't want to prevent you at all. Do you think I am here because I like it? Let me out and I'll go away gladly enough. But as for paying, I wouldn't dream of it, your Honour."

In a sudden access of fury Don Lollo made to give a kick at the jar but stopped in time. Instead he seized it with both hands and shook it violently, uttering a hoarse growl.

"You see what fine cement it is," Zi' Dima remarked from inside.

"You rascal!" roared Don Lollo. "Whose fault is it, yours or mine? You expect me to pay for it, do you? You can starve to death inside first. We'll see who'll win."

He went away, forgetting all about the five lire which he had tossed into the jar that morning. But the first thing Zi' Dima thought of doing was to spend that money in having a festive evening, in company with the farm-hands, who had been delayed in their work by that strange accident, and had decided to spend the night at the farm, in the open air, sleeping on the threshing-floor. One of them went to a neighbouring tavern to make the necessary purchases. The moon was so bright that it seemed almost day—a splendid night for their carousal.

Many hours later Don Lollo was awakened by an infernal din. Looking out from the farm-house balcony, he could see in the moonlight what looked like a gang of devils on his threshing-floor: his men, all roaring drunk, were holding hands and perform-ing a dance round the jar, while Zi' Dima, inside it, was singing at the top of his voice.

This time Don Lollo could not restrain himself, but rushed down like a mad bull and, before they could stop him, gave the jar a push which started it rolling down the slope. It continued on its course, to the delight of the intoxicated company, until it hit an olive tree and cracked in pieces, leaving Zi' Dima the winner in the dispute.

THE MADONNA'S GIFT

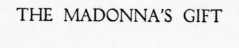

THE MADONNA'S GIFT

+   ASSUNTA
+   FILOMENA
+   CROCIFISSA
+   ANGELICA
+   MARGHERITA
+   . . . .

A CROSS—and opposite the cross the name of the daughter who had died. . . . There were five names in the column, and then a sixth cross, ready for the name of the last daughter—Agatha—whose sufferings would soon come to an end.

Don Nuccio D'Alagna put his fingers in his ears, to keep out the sound of her cough, which came to him from the next room. As if himself attacked by the paroxysm, he blinked his eyes, wrinkling up his haggard, bristly face, and rose to his feet.

He seemed almost lost in his enormous coat. It was a garment whose original ·colour could no longer be discerned, and it showed how charity can play the buffoon when it wishes, for he had un≀

doubtedly received that old coat as a charitable donation. To remedy as far as possible the redundance of the gift, Don Nuccio had rolled up the sleeves several times until they ended at his thin wrists. But, like that coat, everything about him— his utter destitution, his misfortunes, the bareness of that house, so full of light, but also of flies— everything gave the impression of an exaggeration that was hardly credible.

Before going into the next room, he waited for a few moments, knowing that his daughter did not like him to hurry to her immediately after one of those attacks of coughing: he spent the time in obliterating with his finger the graveyard which he had sketched out on the tabletop.

*   *   *   *   *

Apart from the sick girl's wretched pallet, that other room contained only a ramshackle chair and a straw mattress rolled up on the floor which the old man dragged every morning into the next room, and on which, without undressing, he threw himself down to sleep. The walls were covered with paper which had been elegant in its day, but was now faded, torn and hanging in tatters. There were marks on the walls that showed where pieces of furniture, long since sold, had once stood, and the cobwebs they had concealed still clung there.

The light was so bright in that bare, resonant

room that the pale, emaciated face of the sick girl lying on the bed seemed almost to disappear, leaving only the eyes, sunk deep in blue hollows. But, to make up for that, her red hair, spread on the pillow, with the sun shining on to it, seemed like a blazing fire. There she lay, very still now, looking at her hands in the sunshine, or twisting round her fingers the curling ends of that magnificent hair. She was so quiet and still in that empty sunlit room that there was a feeling of unreality, almost of the supernatural about her—or there would have been, but for the buzzing of the flies.

Seated on the only chair, Don Nuccio began to turn over in his mind a very desirable prospect for his daughter, the only desirable prospect remaining for her. He prayed that God would open her eyes, that her terrible suffering, lying there on the foul straw mattress of that bed in the empty house, would induce her to ask to be transferred to the hospital, a place that none of her sisters, who had died before her, had been willing to enter.

One died there just the same? No!—Don Nuccio shook his head conclusively—it was different there—so much cleaner.

In his mind's eye, he had a clear picture of a long, bright ward with a row of innumerable white cots down each side, and a huge window at the end, showing the blue sky. He saw once more the sisters of charity with those big white wings to their hoods and those medals hanging from their rosaries, which clinked together at every step they took. He could see, too, an old priest, who led him by the hand along that ward: dazed by his distress, he peered at one bed after another: at last the priest said to him: "Here", and led him to the side of one of those beds. On it, at the point of death and no longer recognisable, lay the wretched woman, mother of his six daughters, who had run away from his home only to end up in that place. Yes, it was his wife. . . . His eldest daughter, Assunta, had already died, at the age of twelve.

"She took after you. She does not forgive you," he had said.

"Nuccio D'Alagna!" The old priest spoke sharply to him: "We are in God's presence."

"Yes, father. It is God's will, so I forgive her."

"Also in the name of the daughters?"

"One is dead, father. In the name of the five who will follow after her."

*　*　*　*　*

All of them, in fact, died, one after the other; and Don Nuccio had now become almost stupefied. In dying, those five girls had carried off with them his soul—all save a shred of it attached to the last daughter. This shred, however, though only as it were a filament, still remained alight at the tip, burning with a small, bright flame—his faith.

Death, life, mankind, advancing years, all had blown upon it to put it out—they had not suc‹ceeded.

One morning he had seen a neighbour, who lived opposite, open the door of his bird‹cage and drive away a tame chaffinch which Don Nuccio had sold him for a few coppers some days pre‹viously. It was winter and the rain was falling; the poor little bird had come to the windows of his former room and fluttered against them, as if asking for help and hospitality. He had opened the win‹dow—how he had caressed that little head, soaked by the rain! Then the bird had perched on his shoulder, just as it used to do, and had started pecking the lobe of his ear. But why had that neighbour turned it out of the cage? It was not long before Don Nuccio discovered the reason. He had already noticed, some days before, that people avoided him in the street and that those who saw him pass made certain gestures. . . .

The bird had remained in his house throughout the winter, hopping and flying about the two rooms, singing happily, well satisfied with some bread‹crumbs. When the fine weather came, it flew away, but not all at once; first it made little excursions to the roofs of the neighbouring houses, returning at nightfall; then it had gone away for good.

Oh, well! One might turn a bird out. . . . But

to turn him out also, with his daughter at death's door, to throw him into the street—was that conscience?

"As for conscience, Don Nuccio, I've got a conscience. But I'm also the manager of the lottery," was the answer he received from Spiga, who had employed him in his gambling-shop for many years.

Every trade, every profession has its own conscience. If one is a seller of lottery tickets, can one be held to be doing a bad action in taking the bread out of the mouth of an old man who has a reputation in the village of possessing the evil eye, so that he cannot attract clients to try their luck in gambling?

Don Nuccio had to admit the force of that cogent argument and left the shop in tears. It was a Saturday evening. In the house opposite, that same neighbour who had turned the chaffinch out of the cage, was giving a dinner in celebration of his success in the lottery. And it was he, Don Nuccio himself, who had issued the ticket to that neighbour. That was a fine proof of his having the evil eye!

He sat at his window, looking into the house opposite, at the sumptuous feast and the guests chattering as they ate and drank. After a time, one of them rose and banged-to the shutters of the window facing him.

THE MADONNA'S GIFT

Ah well! It was God's will. . . .

*   *   *   *   *

He said it without a shadow of irony—Don
Nuccio D'Alagna—that if all these troubles had
come upon him, it was a sign that it was God's will.
It was his favourite expression and each time he
uttered it, he would roll back his long sleeves until
his thin wrists emerged.

"All nonsense," was however the reply which
always came from Don Bartolo Scimpri, the only
person left who was not afraid to approach him.

Tall as a maypole, big-boned and black as charcoal, Don Bartolo Scimpri still wore a priest's robes,
although he had been excommunicated some years
back. The sleeves of his greasy gown, now green
with age, had the opposite drawback to those of
Don Nuccio's coat, for they only reached a little
below the elbow, leaving his hairy forearms exposed
to view. The hem of his robe revealed not only his
huge feet shod in the heavy boots worn by the
peasants, but often even his sunburnt shins, because
his habit of screwing up his cotton socks tightly at
the top, to make them cling to his calves, invariably ended in their collapsing in tatters on to his
ankles.

He enjoyed boasting of his ugliness, of his forehead, which ran in a straight line from the top of
his bald head right down to the tip of his enormous

nose, giving him the strangest resemblance to a turkey.

"This is the sail," he would exclaim, slapping his forehead. "It fills with the breath of the divine spirit!"

Then, taking his huge nose between two fin, gers:—

"This is the helm!"

And he would give a loud snort and jerk the two fingers away with a flutter, as if they had been scorched.

He was at open warfare with all the clergy, because, as he expressed it, the clergy had crippled God. The devil, on the other hand, had made great progress. At all costs, it was necessary to rejuvenate God, to make Him travel by rail, to bring Him up to date, and have done with all those mysteries, so that He could get ahead of the devil.

"Electric light! Electric light!" he used to shout, waving his long, sleeveless arms. "I know who takes advantage of all this darkness. 'God' means 'Light'."

It was high time to stop all those silly perform, ances of the religious ceremonies—masses and adoration of the Host. He drew a comparison between the priest in his long ceremony of the con, secration of the wafer which he then swallows, and the cat which first plays with the mouse and then devours it.

THE MADONNA'S GIFT

He had founded 'the New Church' and was already engaged in drawing up the articles of the New Faith. He thought them out at night and wrote them down. But first he had to discover the treasure. How? By means of a clairvoyant. He had one, who assisted him in diagnosing illnesses. For Don Bartolo also healed the sick. He healed them with certain decoctions, extracted from special herbs, always in accordance with the instructions of the clairvoyant.

Marvellous cures were ascribed to Don Bartolo, but he was not boastful about them. Bodily health he would restore gratis to anyone who had faith in his method of treatment. He himself set as his goal something quite different—to prepare people for the healing of their souls.

People could not make up their minds whether to look upon him as a madman or a charlatan. Some said one thing, some the other. A heretic he was, for sure, and perhaps possessed by the devil. The hut in which he lived, in his small holding close by the cemetery, above the village, seemed like a wizard's den. Lantern in hand, the peasants from round about would repair there at night, their heads shrouded in the hoods of their cloaks, to obtain information from the clairvoyant as to the exact sites of certain *trovature*—treasures which were said to have been buried in the neighbourhood at the time of the revolution. They shook with fear whilst Don Bartolo, mute and spectral, was hypnotising the clairvoyant, his hands held above her head, in the flickering light of a vegetable⁄oil lamp. They shook with fear, too, when he left the woman asleep in the hut and asked them to come outside with him, and made them kneel down on the bare earth beneath the starry sky. He too knelt down. First he would listen to the subdued night sounds, then say mysteriously:—

"Sssss . . . there it comes! there it comes!"

And, lifting up his head, he improvised strange prayers, which seemed to his audience to be blas⁄phemies and invocations of the devil.

Re⁄entering the hut, he would say:—

"That is how one should pray to God, in His temple, along with the crickets and the frogs."

If a little creaking sound came from the old worm⁄eaten chest that lay like a coffin in the corner of the hut, or if the wick of the oil lamp sputtered at a puff of air, a shudder passed over the watching peasants, who crouched there intent and stiff with fright.

Once the treasure was found, the New Church could be made public; it would be open to the air and sunlight, without altars or images. As to the functions of the New Priests, Don Bartolo came to expound them daily to Don Nuccio D'Alagna— the only person who would listen to him without

protesting or running away with his fingers in his
ears.

He did, however, from time to time venture to
say, with a sigh: "Leave it in God's hands!"

But Don Bartolo inevitably retorted: "All nonsense!"

Out of charity, he gave Don Nuccio the work of
copying, at so much a page, the articles of the New
Faith which he scribbled at night. He also brought
him food and magic drugs for the sick daughter.

As soon as his visitor had left, Don Nuccio would
hurry to the church to ask pardon of God the
Father, Jesus, the Virgin and all the saints, as many
as he had heard of, for all the blasphemies he had
to listen to and for the diabolical stuff he had to
copy in the evening, out of sheer necessity. Had
it been for himself alone, he would rather have died
of starvation; but it was also for his daughter, poor
innocent soul. The devout Christians had all
abandoned her. Could it be the will of God that in
their utter destitution, in the black darkness of
their misery, the only light of charity that shone
upon them should come from that demon garbed
as a priest? What should he do, O Lord, what
should he do? What great sin had he committed,
so that even that mouthful of bread must seem to
him poisoned by the hand that offered it? He
knew that that man exercised a fiendish power over
him.

BETTER THINK TWICE ABOUT IT

"Set me free, O Virgin Mary, set me free from him!"

Don Nuccio knelt on the steps in front of the niche where the Madonna stood. She was decked out with gems and golden coins and she wore a blue silk dress and a white cloak spangled with golden stars. He raised his eyes, brimming over with tears, to the smiling face of the Mother of God. He preferred to address his supplication to her, that by her entreaties she should obtain from God forgiveness for his sins—not so much for the accursed bread which he ate, not so much for the diabolical writings which he had to copy, as for another sin, beyond a doubt the gravest of all. He confessed it in fear and trembling. He had allowed himself to be put to sleep by Don Bartolo, just like the clairvoyant.

The first time, he had done it for his daughter's sake, to find, whilst in the hypnotic trance, the herb which was to cure her. The herb had not been found, but he had continued to allow himself to be hypnotised, in order to feel that new gratification, the beatitude of that strange sleep.

"Let us fly, Don Nuccio, let us fly!" Don Bartolo would say to him, holding his two thumbs, whilst he was already asleep yet still able to see! "Do you feel you have wings? That's right! Then let's have a good flight. I'll show you the way."

The girl, raising herself on one elbow in the bed,

watched the scene, wide-eyed with anxiety and fright: she saw her father's closed eyelids quiver as if he was dazzled by the giddy rapidity of his flight, and had lost his way over an immense glittering expanse.

"Water . . . lots of water . . . lots of water . . ." Don Nuccio murmured with a gasp, and it seemed as if his voice came from very far away.

"We will cross that sea," replied Don Bartolo in a deep voice, his brows knotted as if his will-power was being taxed to the utmost. "We will alight at Naples, Don Nuccio. You'll see what a fine city it is. Then we will continue our flight and go to Rome to worry the Pope, buzzing around him in the form of a blue-bottle." . . .

"O Virgin Mary, O most holy Mother!" Don Nuccio would afterwards pray before her shrine, "set me free from that devil who holds me in his power." . . .

Don Bartolo did indeed hold him in bondage, and only needed to look at him in a certain way, for him to feel at once a curious collapse of all his limbs, and for his eyes to close of their own accord. As he sat at his daughter's bedside, Don Nuccio could always tell by a certain trembling in his body, when Don Bartolo was coming, even before he had so much as set his foot on the staircase.

"Here he is, he's coming," he would say; and shortly after, Don Bartolo would indeed appear and

93

would greet the father and daughter with his deep,
full tones:—

"Benedicite."

* * * * *

"He is coming," said Don Nuccio to his
daughter one day when, after a violent attack of
coughing, she had suddenly felt better, really
relieved, so much so that she had started talking in
a way quite unusual for her, not indeed of getting
well—for she could not deceive herself to that
extent—but of a possible brief respite from the
malady, so that she might leave her bed for a while.

Hearing her speak like that, Don Nuccio felt
himself at death's door. O Virgin Mary! was that
to be her last day? For the other daughters had
also talked like that—"Better, I'm better!"—and
had died soon afterwards. Was this then the free,
dom which the Virgin was granting him? That
was not at all what he had so often prayed for. He
had prayed for his own death, so that his daughter,
finding herself alone, should consent to be taken
to the hospital. Instead of that, was he to be left
alone? Was he to be at the death-bed of that last
child, that poor helpless darling? Was that God's
will?

Don Nuccio clenched his fist: if his daughter was
dying, he had no longer need of anything, or of
any one. All the less, therefore, would he be in

need of the man who, whilst succouring the wants of the body, was damning his soul.

He stood up and pressed his hands hard against his face.

"What's the matter, Papa?" the girl asked in surprise.

"He is coming, he is coming," he replied, as if speaking to himself, and he clenched and unclenched his fists, making no attempt to conceal his agitation.

"Well, what if he *is* coming . . ." said little Agatha with a smile.

"I'm going to kick him out!" and Don Nuccio left the room, determined to do so.

That was what God wished. That was why God left him alive and was taking away his daughter. He wished for a rebellious uprising against the tyranny of that demon. He wished to give him time to repent of his great sin. With these thoughts in his mind, he hurried to meet Don Bartolo and stop him at the entrance.

Don Bartolo was coming quite slowly up the last stairs. He looked up, saw Don Nuccio on the landing at the top, and greeted him as usual:—

"Benedicite."

"Stop! stop!" blurted out Don Nuccio, almost choking with excitement and distress. With arms extended, he stood in front of Don Bartolo and said:—

"To-day the Lord is coming for my daughter."

"Has it come to that?" asked Don Bartolo in a tone of deep sympathy. He attributed the old man's agitation to the imminence of the disaster. "Let me see her."

"No! I tell you!" cried Don Nuccio wildly holding him back by the arm. "In the name of God I say to you, do not go in!"

Don Bartolo looked at him in amazement.

"But why not?"

"Because God commands me thus! Go away! Go away! My soul may be damned, but respect that of an innocent girl, who is soon to appear before the judgment seat of God!"

"Ah! You would turn me out—would you?" said Don Bartolo pointing his forefinger at his breast. "Turn *me* out?" he stormed, drawing him-self up to his full height, and looking in his indig-nation a different person. "So you also, you poor worm, you also, like all this herd of beasts, think me a demon do you? Answer me!"

Don Nuccio leaned back against the wall near the door: he could no longer stand without sup-port: he seemed to become smaller and smaller at each word he heard.

"Ungrateful, low beast!" Don Bartolo continued. "So you also turn against me, following in the footsteps of people who have kicked you for a mangy cur? You bite the hand that has given you bread? I! I have damned your soul! Earth/worm! I would squash you under my feet, if I did not feel such disgust and pity for you! Look me in the eyes! Look at me! Who will keep you from star/vation? Who will pay for your daughter's funeral? Be off, be off to church and ask for the money from your Madonna—your Madonna, all decked out like a loose woman!"

For a long time he stared at him with his terrible eyes; then, as if during that stare he had completed his plans for a savage revenge, he burst into a loud scornful laugh and repeated three times with ever/increasing contempt:—

"Beast! Beast! Beast!"

He turned and went away.

Don Nuccio fell upon his knees, crushed and exhausted. He did not know how long he stayed there on the landing, collapsed like an empty sack. He could not tell how he reached the church and came to the Madonna's shrine. He found himself there, as if in a dream, prostrate, with his face pressed against the steps in front of the niche. He rose to his knees and a flood of words, which scarcely seemed to be his own, burst fervently from his lips:—

"I have suffered so much . . . I have had such troubles and still it is not the end. . . . Holy Virgin, I have always given you praise. That I should die first—no, you did not wish it. . . .

97

BETTER THINK TWICE ABOUT IT

May your holy will be done. Command me, and always, up to the last, I will obey you. I have come here, I have come to offer you with my own hands my last daughter, the last of my blood. Take her to you quickly, O mother of the afflicted. Do not let me have her suffer any longer! I know we are not alone, neither are we abandoned by you. We have your precious aid and in your merciful, blessed hands we place our appeal. O holy hands, O sweet hands, hands that heal every wound, blessed be the head upon which they are placed. If I am not unworthy, those hands will now succour me, will help me to provide for my daughter. O holy Virgin—the candles and the coffin. How shall I provide them? You will provide, O Mother of God! You will provide! Will you? Will you? . . ."

At that moment, in the midst of his delirious prayer, he witnessed a miracle, and a silent smile—almost the smile of one demented—spread over his whole face, transfiguring it.

"Yes?" he asked and then at once shrank back, silent and awed, sitting on his heels, his arms folded across his breast.

For he had seen, in a sudden flash, the smile on the Virgin's face come to life. The smile which had played about her lips now beamed quite life-like from the eyes; and from those lips, though he could hear no voice, he *saw* words come forth:—

"*Take this*".

THE MADONNA'S GIFT

The Virgin moved her hand, from whose fingers dangled a rosary of gold and pearls.

"Take this" the lips repeated still more clearly, for he had remained there as if petrified. Alive, dear God! Alive! Alive! those lips . . . and alive that hand that was urging him with a gesture of invitation. . . . And see! now the head—the head also was moving, urging him to accept the proffered gift. He moved slowly forward. It was as if some outside power was forcing him to extend his trembling hand towards the Madonna's gift. He was just on the point of receiving the rosary when, from the shadow of the other nave, there came a shout like thunder:—

"Thief! Thief!"

Don Nuccio fell back as if struck by lightning.

A man at once ran up, shouting, seized him by the arms and dragged him to his feet, shaking him and handling him roughly.

"You thief! An old man like you stealing! In the Lord's house. . . . Robbing the holy Virgin! Thief! Thief!"

Still screaming at Don Nuccio and spitting in his face, he dragged him towards the door of the church. People loitering in the square rushed to see what was happening and joined in a chorus of abuse, while some of them kicked, struck at, and spat upon the old man, who could only groan and mutter in a demented manner:—

"A gift . . . a gift from the Virgin Mary . . . it was a gift. . . ."

He caught a glimpse of the sun-lit square with the shadow of the cypress tree growing in front of the church, and it seemed to him as if that shadow suddenly rose upright from the square and took on the appearance of a colossal Don Bartolo Scimpri, shaking his head and giving vent to his savage laughter. At the sight, Don Nuccio uttered a scream and fainted in the arms of the people who were dragging him along.

A CALL TO DUTY

A CALL TO DUTY

PAOLINO LOVICO sank on to a stool outside the chemist's shop on the *Piazza Marina*. He took out his handkerchief, mopped up the sweat that trickled out of his hair on to his purple face, looked inside at the counter and asked Saro Pulejo, the chemist:—

"Has he been and gone away again?"

"Gigi? No, but he won't be long now. Why?"

"Why? Because I need his services. Why? . . . You want to know too much!"

He spread his handkerchief over his head and, resting his elbows on his knees and his chin on his hands, sat frowning gloomily at the ground.

Every one on the. *Piazza Marina* knew him. Soon a friend of his passed.

"Hallo! Paoli!"

Lovico raised his eyes but lowered them again promptly muttering:—

"Leave me alone!"

Another friend called out:—

"Paoli, what's the matter?"

This time Lovico snatched his handkerchief from

his head and swung round on his stool until he almost faced the wall.

"Paoli, are you feeling ill?" asked Saro Pulejo from his counter.

"Oh! Go to the devil!" cried Paolino Lovico, rushing into the shop. "It's no business of yours, I tell you. I don't ask *you* any questions, whether you feel well or don't feel well, what illness you've got or haven't got. Leave me alone!"

"Well, well," replied Saro. "You must have been bitten by a tarantula. You asked for Gigi, so I thought that . . ."

"But am I the only person on the face of the earth?" shouted Lovico, with flashing eyes and furious gestures. "Mightn't I have a sick dog—or a turkey with a cough? In the name of all that's good and holy, do get on with your own business!"

"Hallo! There is Gigi!" said Saro, laughing.

Gigi Pulejo entered hurriedly, and went straight across to the box on the wall, to see if there were any urgent messages for him in his pigeon-hole.

"Hallo! Paoli."

"Are you in a hurry?" Paolino Lovico asked, without returning his salutation.

"In an awful hurry," said Dr. Pulejo with a sigh. He pushed his hat on the back of his head and fanned his forehead with his handkerchief. "Nowadays, my dear fellow, there's always a lot of work to get through."

A CALL TO DUTY

"I expected as much," replied Paolino Lovico with an angry sneer. He clenched his fists threateningly and cried:—

"What's the epidemic? Cholera? Plague? Are your patients all being carried off by cancer? Look here! You've got to listen to me. Here I am, as good as dead, and I claim the right of priority. . . . I say, Saro, haven't you any work for your pestle and mortar?"

"No, why?"

"Well, then, we'll go away," replied Lovico, clutching Gigi Pulejo's arm and dragging him outside. "I can't tell you in there."

"Is it a long story?" asked the doctor, when they were in the street.

"Very long!"

"My dear fellow, I'm sorry, but I haven't the time——"

"You haven't the time! D'you know what I am going to do? I'll throw myself under a tram, break my leg and compel you to spend half the day looking after me. . . . Where have you got to call?"

"First of all, close by here, in the *Via Butera*."

"I'll walk there with you," said Lovico. "You go up and pay your visit, and I'll wait down below for you. We can go on with the conversation after you've finished."

"But—I say!—what the devil's the matter?"

asked the doctor, stopping for a moment to stare at his friend.

Under the doctor's scrutiny Paolino Lovico assumed a disconsolate posture. With knees bent and arms hanging limply open, he struck an attitude of the utmost dejection, as he answered:—

"My dear Gigi, I'm done for."

His eyes filled with tears.

"Tell me about it," the doctor urged him. "Let's go on walking. Now then, what *has* happened?"

After a few steps, Paolino stopped and caught hold of the doctor's sleeve, saying with an air of mystery:—

"I speak to you as a brother, remember. Other, wise, not a word. A doctor is like a father,con, fessor, isn't that so?"

"Certainly; we also keep professional secrets."

"Good. Then what I say will be in the strictest secrecy, as if spoken to a priest at confession."

Placing one hand on the pit of his stomach and giving a meaning look, he added solemnly:—

"Silent as the tomb—eh?"

Then he opened his eyes very wide and, holding his thumb and fore,finger together, to give special significance to each word he was to utter, slowly declared:—

"Petella keeps two households."

"Petella?" asked Gigi Pulejo, altogether puzzled. "Who's Petella?"

"Good God! Why, Captain Petella!" exclaimed Lovico. "Petella of the General Steamship Company . . ."

"I don't know the man," said Dr. Pulejo.

"What! You don't know him! Well, so much the better. But as silent as the tomb, all the same, eh? . . . Two households," he repeated with the same tone of intense gloom, "one here—the other in Naples."

"Well?"

"Oh! So you think that's nothing?" asked Paolino Lovico, his face suddenly contorted with anger. "A married man takes a mean advantage of his calling as sailor and establishes a second household in another province, and you think nothing of it! Why, Good God! that's how the Turks behave!"

"Yes, entirely Turkish, I grant you. But what business is it of yours? Where do you come in?"

"How do I come in! What business is it of mine!"

"Yes—excuse my asking—but are you a relation of Petella's wife?"

"No!" shouted Paolino Lovico, his eyes suffused with blood. "The poor woman suffers pitiably! She's a very respectable woman—d'you understand? Most shamefully betrayed by her own husband—d'you understand? Does one need to

107

be related to her, to feel one's blood boil at the treatment?"

"But—excuse me—but what can I do in the matter?" enquired Gigi Pulejo, with a shrug of his shoulders.

"You don't give me a chance of telling you, damn you!" burst out Lovico. "Damn that brute! Damn the weather! How infernally hot it is! I feel as if I'm bursting! . . . Well, look here! Our friend Petella—our very good friend Petella— is not content with betraying his wife and keeping another household over in Naples, but he has three or four children there too, by that woman, while he has only one single child by his wife. He refuses to have any more by her! As for the children over there, you understand, they're illegitimate and so, if he has any more, it doesn't worry him at all—he can discard them, when he wants to. But it's quite a different thing here—if he should have another child by his wife, it would be legitimate, and he could not get rid of it. So what d'you think the dirty swine does?—He's been doing it for the last two years, I tell you—On the days on which he lands here, he deliberately picks a quarrel with his wife, maybe on the most trifling pretext, and, when night comes he shuts himself up in his room and sleeps alone. Next day he starts on his voyage again and leaves all risk behind. It has been going on like that for the past two years."

"Poor lady!" exclaimed Gigi Pulejo, sorry for her, but unable to repress a smile. "Excuse my saying so, however—I still don't understand . . ."

"Listen, dear old Gigi," resumed Lovico, with a change of tone, taking hold of his friend's arm. "For the last four months I have been giving Latin lessons to the boy—Petella's son—who's ten years old and is in the first form."

"Oh!" said the doctor.

"If you only knew how sorry I have felt for that unfortunate lady!" proceeded Lovico. "What tears, what tears the poor woman has shed! How good she is! And she's so handsome too, you see. I mean to say, if she were ugly, you would under⟨ stand . . . but she's so beautiful! To see her treated like that—betrayed, despised, just thrown in a corner like a useless rag! I should like to know who could have held out against such treatment! What woman is there, that wouldn't have rebelled? Who can condemn her? She is *such* a respectable woman—it's absolutely imperative to save her, dear old Gigi. You understand—don't you? She now finds herself in a most unfortunate condition . . . she's in despair about it."

Gigi Pulejo stopped still and looked severely at Lovico.

"No! No! my dear fellow," he said. "Those are things I do not undertake. I don't want to have anything at all to do with the Penal Code."

BETTER THINK TWICE ABOUT IT

"You old fool!" exclaimed Lovico. "What have you got into your head now? What on earth do you imagine I'm wanting you to do? What d'you take me for? Do you think I am a man without any morals,—a ruffian? That I want your assistance to . . . Oh! It makes me quite sick—the mere thought of it!"

"Then what the devil *do* you want from me? I don't understand!" shouted Dr. Pulejo, losing patience.

"I want what is only fair and right!" shouted back Paolino Lovico. "Morality—that's what I want. I want Petella to be a decent husband and not to shut his bedroom door in his wife's face, when he comes ashore here!"

Gigi Pulejo broke out into a fit of hearty laughter.

"Wha . . . What . . . are you ask . . . are you asking . . . ha! ha! ha! ha! that I should do to poor Pe . . . to poor Petella . . . ha! ha! ha! . . . bring the horse to the water and make him drink? . . . ha! ha! ha!"

"That's right! laugh away, you coarse beast," bellowed Paolino Lovico, shaking his fists excitedly. "There's a tragedy coming, and you laugh! He's a rotter who won't do his duty, and you laugh! A woman's honour, her very life at stake, and you laugh! Not to mention myself. I'm as good as dead, I'll throw myself into the sea, if you don't help me—I tell you that!"

"But how can I help?" asked Pulejo, still unable to stop laughing.

Paolino Lovico halted in the middle of the street, with an air of great determination, and seized the doctor firmly by the arm.

"Do you know what's going to happen?" he said gloomily. "Petella arrives this evening and goes off again to-morrow for the Levant; he is bound for Smyrna and will be away for about a month. There's no time to spare! It's got to be done promptly or it will be too late. For heaven's sake, dear Gigi, save me! Save that poor woman he victimises! You must know of some means, of some way out . . . don't laugh, by God! or I'll strangle you! No—I don't mean that—laugh, laugh as much as you like, laugh at my despair, as long as you help me—as long as you provide some means, some way out, some medicine. . . ."

Gigi Pulejo had now reached the house in the *Via Butera* where he had to pay a call. He made a great effort to restrain his laughter and said:—

"In fact, you want me to prevent the captain finding some pretext for starting a quarrel with his wife to-night?"

"Exactly!"

"In the name of morality—isn't that so?"

"In the name of morality—are you still joking?"

"No! no! I'm quite serious. Now, listen! I'm going upstairs; you go back to the chemist's—

to Saro's—and wait there for me. I'll be back soon."

"But what are you going to do?"

"You leave that to me," said the doctor reassur‹ ingly. "Go back to Saro's and wait for me there."

"Be quick then," shouted Lovico after him, holding up his hands in supplication.

* * * * *

Towards sunset, Paolino went to the Scalo pier to see Captain Petella arrive, with his boat—the Segesta. He could not exactly say why, but he felt that he must see him, even if only from a dis‹ tance—see how he looked and send a string of silent oaths in his direction. He had hoped that, after succeeding in his appeal for Dr. Pulejo's assistance, the excitement which had tortured him all the morning would show signs of subsiding; but not a bit of it! He had conveyed a mysterious cream‹puff to the Signora Petella—the captain was so fond of pastry—and had left her house and started wandering aimlessly about, and all the time his feeling of excitement had grown stronger and stronger.

And now it was evening. But he wanted to put off going to bed for as long as possible. He soon tired, however, of drifting about the town, and his worry grew with the fear that he might start a quarrel with any one of his numberless acquaintances who might be so ill-advised as to address him. For he had the misfortune to be a man with an entirely transparent disposition. That was the trouble! And this transparence of his was a source of endless merriment to all those others, those hypocrites, who went about cloaked in lies. It was as if the sight of passions all exposed and naked— even the saddest and most painful passions—could only inspire laughter in other people: either they never had experienced them, or they were so used to concealing them, that they could no longer recognise genuine feeling in a poor fellow, like himself, who had the misfortune of being unable to conceal or control his passions.

He returned home, and threw himself down on his bed, without undressing.

How pale she was, how pale that poor darling was, when he had handed her the pastry! So pale and eyes so clouded by worry that she really wasn't beautiful. . . .

"Look cheerful, dearest," he had urged her in a choking voice. "Get yourself up nicely, whatever you do! Wear that Japanese silk blouse which suits you so well . . . and above all, I implore you, do not let him find you down in the dumps, like this . . . be brave, come, be brave! Is everything in order? Remember, don't give him any possible ground for complaint! Courage, darling! Goodbye, till to-morrow. We'll hope that all will go

well. . . . And please don't forget to hang out a
handkerchief as a signal, on that cord there, in
front of your bedroom window. The first thing I
shall think of doing to-morrow is to come and
see it. . . . Do let me have that signal, darling,
do!"

Before leaving her house, he had made blue-
pencil marks, 'ten' and 'ten with credit' against
the Latin translations in the son's exercise book: the
lad, who was never very bright, was now in a state
of panic.

"Nono, show that to Papa. . . . See how pleased
he'll be! Go on like that, my lad, go on like that
and in a few days you'll know more Latin than one
of the geese of the Capitol—you know, one of those
geese that put the Gauls to flight. Three cheers for
Papirius! Be gay! We must all be bright and
cheerful this evening, Nono—Papa is coming! Be
cheery and good! Clean and well-behaved! Let
me look at your nails . . . are they clean? That's
right. Take care not to dirty them. Three cheers
for Papirius, Nono, three cheers for him!"

How about the pastry? Could that ass Pulejo
have been fooling him? No, no, impossible! He
had clearly explained to the doctor how grave the
position was: it would be a shameless rascality for
his friend to deceive him. But . . . but . . . but
. . . how if the remedy wasn't as efficacious as the
doctor said?

A CALL TO DUTY

The indifference, and indeed the positive con,
tempt, of that fellow for his own wife now made
him seethe with rage, as if it were a personal
affront to himself. Indeed it was! To think that
the woman with whom he, Paolino Lovico, was
satisfied,—nay more than satisfied—whom he
thought so eminently desirable, should be held of
no account by a low swine like that! It almost
looked as if he, Paolino Lovico, were quite content
with another man's leavings, with a woman who
had no value to another man. . . . What! The
Neapolitan lady better than the wife—more
beautiful? How he would have liked to see her,
put her alongside the other, point them both out
to the captain and shout in his face: "So you
prefer the other! That's because you're a brute
beast without judgment or taste! As if your wife
isn't worth infinitely more than the other woman!
Just look at her! Look at her well! How can you
have the heart to keep away from her? You just
don't know her attractions . . . you don't appre,
ciate her delicate beauty, the charm of her mel,
ancholy grace! You're an animal, a low pig, and
you can't understand such things; that's why you
despise them. And, after all, how can you make
any comparison between a wretched paramour and
a real lady, a highly respectable woman?"

What a night he passed—not a wink of sleep!
. . . When at last it seemed to him that the sky

was paling, he could no longer lie there, tossing about: it occurred to him that, as the Signora's bed was in a separate room from that of her husband, she might well have hung the handkerchief on the window-cord during the night, so as to allay his anxiety as soon as possible. She must have known that he would not close his eyes all night long, and that, the moment dawn appeared, he would come to look. With this in mind, he hurried to Petella's house, buoyed up by his ardent wish, almost convinced that he would see the signal at the window. His failure to find it there was a terrible blow: his legs tottered under him. Nothing! Nothing! How gloomy the house looked with its Venetian blinds all drawn, as if awaiting a funeral. . . .

A savage idea suddenly assailed him—to go up, rush into Petella's room and strangle him in his bed. Then, all at once, he felt exhausted, ready to drop, as flabby as an empty sack—just as if he really had gone up and committed the crime. He tried to console himself by the reflection that perhaps it was still too early, perhaps he was asking for too much—expecting her to get up in the middle of the night and hang out the signal, so that he should find it there at dawn; perhaps she hadn't been able to manage it, for some reason.

Come, come! It was not yet time for despair; he would wait . . . wait there, however, he could not:

116

every minute would seem an eternity. But his legs . . . what was happening? . . . He seemed to be losing the use of his legs.

As luck would have it, in the first alley into which he turned, he found a café open, a humble restaurant patronised in the early morning by labourers from the docks close by. He entered and collapsed on to a wooden bench.

No one was to be seen, not even the proprietor, but he could hear people talking as they worked, in a dark back room—perhaps they were just beginning to light the fires there.

After a short interval, a rough-looking man in his shirt-sleeves made his appearance, and asked him for his order. Paolino Lovico stared at him with angry surprise, then said:—

"A handker . . . No! I mean . . . a cup of coffee. Strong coffee, very strong, please."

It was soon brought; he took a gulp—half of it went down, the rest spurted from his mouth, as he sprang to his feet. Good Heavens! The stuff was boiling hot!

"What's the matter, Sir?"

"Oh . . . oohh!" groaned Lovico, his eyes and mouth stretched to their widest capacity.

"Some water, a sip of water," suggested the restaurant-keeper. "Come, take a drink of water."

"My trousers!" wailed Paolino, looking down at them.

He took out his pocket handkerchief, dipped one corner of it in the glass, and started rubbing the stain briskly. Anyhow the damp felt good to his scalded thigh.

He spread out the wet handkerchief, then at the sight of it grew pale, threw two coppers on the tray and hurried away. But hardly had he turned the corner from the alley, when he found himself face to face with Captain Petella.

"Hallo! You here?"

"Yes, I . . . I . . ." stammered Paolino Lovico, feeling as if he had lost his very last drop of blood, "I . . . I . . . got up early . . . and . . ."

"Went for a walk in the cool of the morning, eh?" said Petella, finishing the sentence for him. "Lucky man! No troubles . . . no worries . . . free! a bachelor!"

Lovico looked closely into his eyes to discover whether . . . Yes . . . it looked like it. . . . The fact that the beast was out of doors at that hour, and that he wore that dark, stormy look . . . meant that he must have quarrelled with his wife again last night. "I'll kill him!" thought Lovico. "On my word of honour I'll kill him!" He managed to answer, however, with a polite smile:—

"But I see that you too . . ."

"I?" growled Petella. "What?"

"You too . . . up so early . . ."

"Oh! You're wondering why you see me out so

118

early? I've had a bad night, Professor. Perhaps it was the heat. . . . I don't know——"

"What, you didn't . . . didn't . . . sleep well?"

"I haven't slept at all," cried Petella in a tone of exasperation. "You see, when I don't sleep, when I don't even doze at all, I get very angry."

"But . . . excuse me . . . what fault . . ." stammered Lovico, trembling violently but still contriving to smile. "What fault is it of other people, if you won't mind my asking . . ."

"Other people?" enquired Petella, surprised. "What on earth have other people to do with it?"

"Why, you said you got very angry. Angry with whom? Whom do you quarrel with, when the weather's hot?"

"I lose my temper with myself, with the weather, with everybody," exclaimed Petella. "I want air . . . I'm accustomed to the sea. As for the land, Professor, especially in summer-time, I can't stand it, with its houses . . . walls . . . worries . . . and women."

"I'll kill him—on my word of honour I will!" Lovico muttered to himself. He continued to smile slightly, as he spoke:—

"You can't stand women either?"

"Oh! women. . . . Well really, as far as I'm concerned, women . . . you know, my ship moves on and I'm away from them for such a long time. I'm not talking about now, when I'm an old man;

but when I was young—well yes, they did appeal to me. However, one thing I can claim in my favour—I've always retained control over myself; when I want to, I go after them, and when I don't want to, I don't go after them."

"Always?" (I'll kill him!)

"Always, if I want to—you understand. With you it's different, eh? You let yourself be easily caught? A bit of a smile or a gesture, a modest look or a timid one—isn't that so? Come, tell me the truth."

Lovico stood still and looked him in the face, saying:—

"Shall I tell you the truth? Well, if I had a wife . . ."

"But we are not talking of *wives* at the moment. What have wives got to do with it? I said 'women', 'women'!" and Petella burst out laughing.

"Aren't wives women, then? What else are they?"

"Oh yes! They're women all right . . . sometimes! But you haven't got a wife at present, my dear Professor, and I hope for your own sake, that you'll never have one. Wives, you see . . ."

He took his companion's arm and talked and talked and talked. Lovico trembled with anxiety, as he studied the captain's face, noticed his puffy eyes with bluish rings round them and thought that perhaps they looked like that because he had been unable to sleep . . . perhaps. . . . Yet now and again, from some word or other, it really looked as if . . . as if . . . the poor woman was saved. At other moments, he was filled with doubt and even despair. His torture seemed to last for ages, and that brute wanted to walk on and on, and took him the whole way along the sea front. At last he turned to go back to his house.

"I won't leave him," thought Lovico. "I'll go up to his house with him and, if he hasn't done his duty, this'll be the last day of life for all three of us."

He was so absorbed in his murderous intention, so filled with passionate hatred, that it seemed as if his limbs had become disjointed and fallen apart when, turning the corner, he raised his eyes to the window of Petella's house—and saw, hanging from the cord, Oh Lord! one . . . two . . . three . . . four . . . five handkerchiefs!

His nose wrinkled, his mouth fell open, and his head went round, as he gasped in a paroxysm of joy that all but choked him.

"What's the matter?" cried Petella, holding him up.

"Dear Captain!" said Lovico, "dear Captain! thank you! thank you so much! Oh . . . it's given me such pleasure, this . . . this . . . delightful walk . . . but I'm tired . . . dead-tired . . . I'm dropping, really dropping. Thanks, ever so many thanks, dear Captain. Good-bye! A pleasant voyage to you! Good-bye! Thank you! Thank you!"

No sooner had Petella entered his door than Lovico hurried excitedly down the street, uttering loud shouts of joy; with broad grin and bright, exultant eyes, he displayed the five fingers of his hand to everyone he met.

THE CAPTIVE

THE CAPTIVE

IT looked as if old Vicè Guarnotta were walking along the road—so regularly did his body sway from side to side with the movements of the little donkey on which he sat. His legs dangled outside the stirrups and nearly dragged along the dusty highway. He was returning, as he did every day at that hour, from his holding on the edge of the plateau, almost overhanging the sea. The aged donkey, even more tired and melancholy than her master, had begun to pant from the effort of ascend‹ ing the interminable road, which wound its way up the mountain in a succession of steep curves and hair‹pin bends. At the summit of the spur stood the ramshackle houses of the little town, huddled closely together, one above another. It was so late that the peasants had all returned home from the country‹side and the road was deserted. If Guar‹ notta did happen to meet anyone, he always received a friendly greeting, for—God be thanked —they all thought well of him.

In the old man's eyes, the whole world was now as lonely as that highway, and his own life grey as that twilight. He glanced at the bare branches projecting over the low, cracked walls, the tall dusty cacti, and the heaps of road-metal lying here and there—which some one really might have thought of spreading over the numerous holes and ruts. Everything about him was still, silent and deserted, as if, like him, oppressed by a sense of infinite boredom and futility. Even the silence seemed to have turned into dust—dust that lay so thick that he could not hear the footsteps of his donkey.

What quantities of that road-dust had the old man carried home every evening! Whenever he took off his coat, his wife seized it and held it out at arm's length. To relieve her feelings, she displayed it round the room—to the chairs and the wardrobe, the bed and the coffer, exclaiming:—

"Just look at it! Look! Why, you could write on it with your finger!"

If only he would yield to her persuasion and not wear his black suit of broad-cloth out on the farm. Hadn't she ordered three corduroy suits for him, for that very purpose—three of them? And while she raged and angrily gesticulated, Guarnotta, sitting in his shirt-sleeves, often felt tempted to sink his teeth into the three stumpy fingers which she brandished in front of his eyes; but, like a well-behaved dog, he confined himself to giving her a side-glance of dissatisfaction and let her continue her nagging. Fifteen years before—on the death of his only son—had he not vowed that he would dress in black for the rest of his life? So, therefore . . .

"But why d'you want to wear black out in the fields? I'll put crepe bands on the sleeves of your corduroy coats. That and a black tie will be quite enough—after fifteen years!"

He let her nag. Was he not out on his holding by the sea the whole blessed day? For years past, he had never been seen in the town. Therefore, if he did not wear mourning for his son out on the country-side, where was he to wear it? Why, in God's name, didn't she think a little before opening her mouth—then she would leave him in peace. . . . Oh! so he was to wear mourning in his heart, was he? Indeed! And who said that he didn't wear it in his heart? But he wanted people to see some external sign of it. Let the trees see it, and the birds of the air—since the boy, alas! was unable to see that he wore it for him. . . . Why on earth was his wife grumbling so about it? Was it because she had to shake and brush the clothes every evening? Why not let the servants do it? There were three of them to wait upon only two persons. Was it for economy's sake? Come, what nonsense! One black suit a year cost only eighty or ninety lire. She ought to realise that it wasn't

127

right—it wasn't kind of her to go on like that. She was his second wife: the son, who had died, had been by the first one. He had no other relatives— even distant ones; therefore, on his death, all his property (and it was no small amount) would pass to her and to her nephews and nieces. She should keep quiet then, if only for decency's sake. . . . Ah well! Being the sort of woman she was, she didn't, of course, see it in that way.

So that was why he stayed out all day, alone on his land, alone with his trees and the panorama of the sea spread just below him; and, as he listened to the continuous gentle rustling of the foliage and the sad little song of the waves—which seemed to float up to him from an endless distance—his soul was constantly oppressed by a sense of the vanity of all things and the insufferable boredom of life.

* * * * *

He had reached a point less than half-a-mile from the little town and could hear the soft chimes of the *Ave Maria* from the chapel of the *Addolorata* on the top of the hill, when, at a sharp bend in the road, there came a shout:—

"Face to the ground!"

Three men, who had lain ambushed in the shadow, sprang out upon him; he noticed that they wore masks and carried guns. One seized his ass's bridle, while the others, in the twinkling of an eye, dragged him from the saddle and threw him on the road; one man knelt on his legs and fastened his wrists together, the other meanwhile bandaging his eyes with a folded handkerchief tied tightly round his head.

He had barely time to say: "But what do you want, my lads?"—when he was forced to his feet, pushed and hustled off the road, and dragged violently down the stony hill,side towards the valley.

"But, my lads . . ."

"Silence or you're a dead man!"

He was frightened by their rough handling, but still more so by the state of terror that the three men were in—obviously on account of their deed of violence. He could hear them panting like wild beasts. They were going to do something horrible to him. . . .

But perhaps they did not mean to kill him—at any rate not at once. If they had been paid to murder him, or were carrying out a vendetta, they would have despatched him up there on the high, road, from their ambush in the shadows. So it must be that they were carrying him off for a ransom.

"My lads . . ."

They gripped his arms more tightly, shook him, and told him again to be silent.

"But at least loosen the bandage a little. It's very tight on my eyes. . . . I can't . . ."

"Go on! Move. . . ."

First down, then up, now straight on, then turn‹ ing back: down again, then up and up and up. Where could they be taking him?

Sinister imaginings haunted his mind on that terrible, blind march over rocks and thorns, pushed and pulled along in total darkness. And then, suddenly, he saw the lights—the lights of the little town on top of the ridge—the oil lamps shining from the houses and streets—just as he had seen them round the bend a moment before he was attacked, just as he had seen them again and again on his way home from his holding at that evening hour. How strange! He saw them plainly through the tight bandage over his eyes—as clearly as before when his eyes were open. How strange. . . . As he stumbled on and on, savagely pulled and pushed by his captors, so that his heart filled with terror, he took the little lamps with him; and not only those soft, sad little lamps, but the whole of the mountain spur with the town on its summit— the town whose other inhabitants went safely and peacefully about their business, unconscious of his horrible adventure.

At one point he caught the sound of the hurried patter of his ass's hoofs.

Oh! So they were dragging his weary old

donkey along, too! She, poor beast, could not understand. All she would notice would be the unwonted hurry and rough treatment, but she would go where she was taken, without any idea of what had happened. If only they would stop a moment and let him speak, he would tell them quietly that he was ready to pay whatever they demanded. He had not long now to live, and it really was not worth while suffering such hideous treatment just for the sake of a little money—money which brought him no satisfaction.

"My lads . . ."

"Silence! Go on!"

"I can't manage it. . . . Why are you doing this to me? I'm ready to . . ."

"Silence! We'll talk later. Go on!"

They made him trudge like that for what seemed eternity. At last, overcome by weariness and sick and giddy from the tight bandage, he fainted and remained unconscious.

*   *   *   *   *

He recovered his senses next morning and found himself lying, utterly exhausted, in a low cavern.

A strong, musty smell seemed to emanate from the first light of dawn, which entered wanly through the winding entrance to the chalky grotto. Faint though it was, that light comforted him in his pain—the pain he felt from the rough handling he had undergone. He remembered that brutal violence as if it had been a nightmare—remembered how, when he had been unable to keep on his feet, he had been carried, first on one man's back and then on another's, dropped on the ground and dragged along, then held up by his arms and legs.

Where was he now? He listened attentively: from the stillness outside, he imagined that he was high on some lofty peak. The idea made him feel quite giddy. He was unable to move, for his hands and feet were tied, and he lay stretched on the ground like a dead animal. His limbs and head were so heavy that they seemed made of lead. He wondered whether he was wounded. Perhaps they had left him there for dead.

No. There they were, discussing something outside the cave. So his fate was not yet settled. . . . He considered what had happened, and found that he had no longer any thought of attempting to escape from his position of danger. He knew that he could not escape, and he had almost lost the will to do so. The disaster was accomplished—it was as if it had happened a long time ago, almost in a previous life. That life had been a miserable affair, and he had left it far, far away, down below in the valley, where they had captured him. Now he had only the silence of that high place—a void in which the past was forgotten. Even if they set him free, he no longer had the strength, perhaps not even the desire, to go down and restart the old life.

Suddenly a wave of self-pity swept over him, and he began to shudder with horror at the fate awaiting him, as he saw one of his captors crawling into the cave on all fours. The man's face was concealed by a red handkerchief with holes made in front for the eyes. Guarnotta looked quickly at his hands. They carried no weapon, only a new pencil —the kind you buy for a halfpenny—not yet sharpened. In his other hand was a crumpled sheet of common note-paper, with an envelope held in its fold.

The old man felt reassured. He smiled involuntarily. At that moment, the other two—also masked—entered the cave on their hands and knees. One of them came up to him and undid his hands, but not his feet. Then the first to enter spoke:—

"Now have some sense! You must write as we tell you."

Guarnotta thought he recognised the voice. Yes, of course! It was Manuzza—so-called because he had one arm shorter than the other. But was it really he? A glance at the man's left arm confirmed his suspicion. He felt sure that he would recognise the other two, if they removed their masks, for he knew everyone in the town. He replied:—

"Have some sense, indeed! It's you, my lads, who ought to have some sense. To whom do you want me to write? And what am I to write with? That thing?"

He pointed to the pencil.

"Why not? It's a pencil, isn't it?"

"Yes, it's a pencil, all right. But you don't even understand how such things are used."

"What d'you mean?"

"Why! You must sharpen it first!"

"Sharpen it?"

"Yes, sharpen it, with a pen-knife, there—at the tip."

"Pen-knife—I haven't got one," said Manuzza, and added: "Have some sense, now—here, have some sense!" followed by a string of oaths.

"Yes, I've got sense, all right, Manuzza. . . ."

"Oh!" shouted the fellow. "So you've recog-nised me?"

"What else can you expect, when you hide your face and leave your left arm exposed? Take off that handkerchief and look me straight in the eyes. Why are you doing this . . . to me?"

"Stop all that chatter!" bellowed Manuzza, pull-ing the handkerchief from his face. "I've told you to have some sense. Either you write or I'll kill you!"

134

"Yes, yes! I'm ready to write," rejoined Guar‹
notta, "when you've sharpened the pencil. But—
if you don't mind my asking—it's money you
want, my lads, isn't it? How much?"

"Three thousand florins!"

"Three thousand? That's no small sum."

"You're worth that much! Let's have no non‹
sense about it!"

"Three thousand florins?"

"Yes, and more too! More than that!"

"Quite true. I am worth more than that, but
I've not got that sum at home, in ready money. I
should have to sell some houses and fields. D'you
think that can be done at a day's notice and without
my presence there?"

"Tell them to borrow the money!"

"Tell who?"

"Your wife and nephews!"

Guarnotta smiled bitterly and tried to raise him‹
self up on one of his elbows.

"That's just the point I wanted to explain," he
answered. "My lads, you have made a great mis‹
take. Are you counting on my wife and her
nephews? If you're bent on killing me, kill me.
Here I am! Kill me and no more said about it.
But if it's money you're after, you can only get the
money from me, on condition that you let me
return home."

"What are you talking about? Let you go

home? Do you think we're mad? You're joking!"

"Well, then . . ." began Guarnotta, with a sigh.

Manuzza snatched the sheet of writing paper angrily from his companion's hand and repeated:—

"Stop all that chatter, as I told you—just you write! The pencil. . . . Oh God, yes! . . . it has to be sharpened. . . . How's that done?"

Guarnotta explained the way and the men exchanged glances and left the cave. As he saw them crawl out, on all fours—looking like three animals —he could not refrain from smiling once more. He reflected that they were now engaged in trying to sharpen that pencil, and that perhaps, by dint of pruning it like a branch of a tree, they would fail in their attempts. That was what might well happen, and he smiled at the idea, at the thought that, at that moment, his life depended on the absurd difficulty which those three men would be up against, in trying to carry out an operation they had never performed before. Perhaps, when they saw the pencil growing smaller and smaller, they would be so annoyed that, on their next entry, they would show him that though their knives might be no good for sharpening a pencil, they were quite good for cutting his throat. . . . He had been a fool and had committed an unpar-

donable mistake in letting that fellow Manuzza
know that he recognised him. . . . Yes, he could
hear them all talking at once—outside the cave,
shouting and cursing. He was sure they were
passing that wretched halfpenny pencil from one
to another and that it was growing shorter and
shorter under their clumsy treatment. Heaven
knows what kind of knives they held in their
great chalky fists. . . . There they were, crawl*
ing back in single file, having failed in their en*
deavour.

"The wood's rotten," said Manuzza. "That pen*
cil's no good. As *you* know how to write, haven't
you by any chance got a decent pencil in your
pocket, properly sharpened?"

"No, I haven't, my lads," replied Guarnotta.
"And anyhow it would be useless, I assure you. I
would have written if you'd given me a pencil and
paper. But to whom should I write? To my wife
and nephews? They are her nephews, not mine—
d'you understand that? You may be quite sure
that none of them would have answered. They'd
have pretended that they never received the
threatening letter, and wash their hands of me. If
you want money from them, you shouldn't have
begun by falling on me. You should have gone
and made terms with them—say a thousand florins
—for killing me. But they wouldn't even have
paid that much. . . . I quite admit that they look

forward to my death, but—you see—I'm an old man, and they expect that God will very soon grant it to them free of expense and in that way there'll be no feeling of remorse. You surely don't imagine they'd pay you a centesimo, one single centesimo, to *save* my life? You have muddled the whole business. My life is only of interest to myself; and it isn't of much interest even to me—that's the truth. Still, I admit, I don't want to die like this— it's a horrible death. And therefore, simply to escape that kind of end, I promise and swear to you, by the soul of my dear son, that, as soon as I possibly can—within two or three days—I myself will bring you the money to the place you appoint."

"Yes! After you've already reported us!"

"I swear that I will not do so. I swear that I will not breathe a word of this matter to anyone. Remember, my life is at stake!"

"It is at present, but will it be when you are free? Why, even before going home, you'll report us to the police!"

"I swear to you that I will not! You really ought to trust me. Remember that I go out every day into the country, and my life, out there, is in your hands. And have I not always been a father to you boys? God knows, you have always looked up to me and respected me. . . . Do you think that I'm anxious to expose myself to the danger of a vendetta? No, you ought to trust my word and let me return home, and you can be sure that you'll have the money."

They said no more to him, but exchanged glances and left the cave, crawling away on hands and knees.

* * * * *

All day long he did not see them again. At first he could hear them engaged in discussion outside; after a while, no further sound reached him.

He lay there, turning over in his mind all the probabilities, and wondering what decision they would come to. One thing seemed clear to him— that he had fallen into the hands of three stupid fellows, mere amateurs, and that this was probably their first essay in crime. They had entered on it blindly, thinking solely of his money, without giving any previous consideration to their position as married men with families. Now that they realised their blunder, they did not know what to do next, and could see no way out of their difficulties. As for his oath that he would not denounce them, none of the three would trust in it, least of all Manuzza, who had been recognised. What was to happen then?

His only hope was that it would not occur to any one of them to feel repentance for their stupid, unreasonable act, and a consequent desire to wipe out every trace of this first offence. If they decided to continue brigandage as outlaws, they might as well spare his life and set him free, without worry‹ ing about his denouncing them; but, if they repented and wanted to return to an honest liveli‹ hood, they must necessarily prevent the denun‹ ciation which they were convinced would follow on his freedom, and therefore they must murder him.

It followed from this that God might, he hoped, come to his assistance by enlightening them—by bringing them to see that it would not profit them to live an honest life. It should not be difficult to persuade them of this, seeing that they had already shown, by kidnapping him, that they were prepared to imperil their immortal souls. But he was very anxious about the disillusionment which they must have experienced when their eyes were opened to the great blunder they had committed, at the outset of a career of crime: for disillusion‹ ment is very apt to turn into repentance and into a desire to abandon a path which has begun badly. To withdraw from it, obliterating every trace of their previous steps, they might logically hold that they had no alternative but to commit a crime; for, if they were willing to set him free, would they not, with equal logic, be forced to go on committing crimes? They would conclude then that it was better to commit that one crime at the outset—a deed which would remain secret, entirely untraced—than to commit any number of crimes, done openly as outlaws. At the cost of one misdeed, they could still hope to save themselves, not indeed as far as their consciences were concerned, but in the sight of men: if they were to release him—they would argue—they would be irretrievably lost.

As a result of these harassing reflections, he arrived at the conclusion that on that day or on the morrow, perhaps that very night while he slept, they would assassinate him.

* * * * *

He waited until it grew dark inside the cave. Then, overcome with terror at the thought of falling asleep in that silent and dreadful place, he determined to crawl outside the cave, even though his hands and feet were still tied. He moved forward with infinite difficulty, wriggling along like a worm, restraining his instinctive fears in an endeavour to make the least possible noise. What could he possibly hope for, in trying to poke his head out, like a glow-worm from its hole? Nothing. But at least he would see the sky and meet his death in the open, face to face, and not have it come upon him treacherously in his sleep. That was something.

141

Ah! there he was, at last. . . . Quietly. . . .
Was that moonlight? Yes, there was the young
moon, and countless stars. . . . What a splendid
night! Where was he? . . . On some mountain﹐
top—the air and the silence proved that. . . .
Perhaps that was Monte Caltafaraci over there, or
San Benedetto. . . . Then what was that valley?
Either the plain of Consolida or the valley of
Clerici? Yes, and that mountain to the west must
be the Carapezza. But if so, what were those twink﹐
ling lights over there, glittering like clusters of
fire﹐flies in the opal moonlight? Were they the
lights of Girgenti? Why then—Good God!—then
he was quite near! And it had seemed as if they
had made him walk so far, so far. . . .

He looked anxiously round him, as if the possi﹐
bility that they might have gone off, leaving him
there, aroused his fear rather than hope. Dark and
motionless, squatting like a great owl on a bank of
chalk, sat one of the three men, left on guard; he
showed plainly in the faint, pale light of the moon.
Was he asleep?

The old man tried to squirm his way out a
little farther, but all at once his arms lost all
their power, as he heard a voice saying quite
calmly:—

"I'm watching you, Don Vicè. Back you go, or
I shoot!"

He held his breath and lay motionless, looking

out. Perhaps the man might think that he had
made a mistake.

"I am watching you."

"Let me have a breath of fresh air," he then
begged. "I'm suffocated inside there. D'you mean
to keep me like this? I'm thirsty—I'm dying of
thirst——"

The man made a threatening gesture:—

"Well, you can stay there, but only on condition
you don't utter a sound. I'm hungry and thirsty
too, as well as you. Keep silent or I make you go
back inside."

Silence. . . . But at least he had the moon,
revealing all those quiet valleys and mountains . . .
and the relief of the fresh air . . . and the sad
glimmer of those distant lights shining from his
native town.

Where had the other two gone? Had they left
to this third man the task of despatching him
during the night. If so, why did he not do it at
once? What was he waiting for? Was he perhaps
waiting for the other two to come back that
night?

Again he felt tempted to speak, but restrained
himself. Well, if that was what they had decided
to do . . .

He looked again at the bank where the man had
been squatting and saw that he had resumed his
former position. Judging from his voice and accent,

Guarnotta concluded that he came from Grotte, a large village among the sulphur mines. Could it possibly be Fillico, a quiet, kindly fellow, a regular beast of burden, strong as a horse. If it really was he—if that silent, hard-working man had left the straight path, it was a bad business.

He could not stand it any longer, but spoke almost automatically, not as a question, in fact without any clear intention—it seemed as if he meant the name to sound as if uttered by some one else:—

"Fillico. . . ."

The man did not stir.

Guarnotta waited, then repeated it in the same tone, as if it were some other person talking; as he spoke, he gazed intently at his finger with which he was drawing marks on the sand.

"Fillico."

This time a shudder ran down his spine at the thought that his obstinacy in repeating that name— almost involuntarily—was likely to be paid for by a gunshot in return.

But again the man made no movement. Then Guarnotta gave a loud sigh of despair; suddenly his head was a dead weight which he could no longer support. He lay like a dying animal, with his face in the sand—the sand running into his open mouth—and, in spite of the prohibition against speaking and the threat of shooting, he began to rave—to rave interminably. He spoke of the beautiful moon—he cried a farewell to it, for it had by this time set—; he spoke of the stars which God had created and placed in the distant heavens, so that the brute creation could not know that they were really countless worlds, much larger than this earth; he spoke of the earth, saying that everyone who is not a brute—a mere animal—knows that it spins like a top; it seemed to relieve his feelings to declare that at that very moment there were men on it with their heads pointing downwards, and that they did not fall off into the sky for reasons which everyone ought to take the trouble to find out, unless he were the lowest of the low—a mere clod into which our Lord God has not breathed the divine spirit.

In the midst of all his wild raving, he suddenly found that he was talking astronomy, expounding it like a professor; and the man, who had gradually drawn nearer to him, was now sitting beside him there, close to the mouth of the cave; and that it actually was as he had guessed—Fillico from Grotte; and that it so happened that Fillico had wanted to know about these matters for many years—all about the zodiac, the milky way, the nebulæ. . . . But he was not easy to convince; he did not think the explanations given were true.

It was a strange situation. It was strange, too,

that though he was at the end of his strength, exhausted by despair, though he had a gun-barrel pointing at him—yet he was able to devote great attention to cleaning his finger-nails with a stalk of grass, taking care that it did not break or bend. He also examined his remaining teeth—only three incisors and one canine—and devoted much consideration to the problem whether his neighbour, the maker of wine-jars, who had lost his wife a fortnight back, was left with three children or with four. . . .

"Now, let's talk seriously. Just tell me, what d'you think I am? By the Madonna! D'you think I am a blade of grass—that blade of grass, there, which you can pluck like this, just as if it were nothing? Feel me! By the Madonna, I'm made of flesh and blood, and I have a soul, which God gave me, just as He has given you one. Yet you mean to cut my throat while I'm asleep? No . . . don't go. . . . Wait here . . . listen to me . . . what? You're not going? Oh! I see—as long as I was speaking of the stars. . . . Listen to what I've got to say. Cut my throat here while I'm awake—not treacherously while I'm asleep. . . . D'you hear? What d'you say to that? You won't answer? But why are you putting it off? What are you waiting for, I want to know? If it's money you're after, you won't get it. You can't keep me here and you don't want to let me go. . . . You mean to kill me? Well, for God's sake do it and get it over!"

But he was talking to empty space. The man had gone off and was again squatting like an owl on the bank, to show him that it was quite useless to speak on that subject—he would not listen to a word.

After all, thought Guarnotta, how stupid it was to worry like that. If he had to be murdered, was it not better to be murdered during his sleep? He even decided that if he was still awake when he heard them crawl into the cave later on, he would shut his eyes and pretend to be sleeping. Not that there was any need to shut his eyes, really—it would be dark and he could keep them open. All he had to do was to make no movement when they came close and were feeling for his throat, to cut it like a sheep's.

So he simply said "Good-night" and crawled away inside the cave.

*   *   *   *   *

They did not, however, murder him. They admitted their blunder; but were unwilling either to set him free or to kill him. They would keep him there.

"What! For ever?"

For as long as God saw fit. They placed them-selves in His hands. The captivity would terminate sooner or later, according as He wished to impose upon them a short or a long expiation for their fault in taking Guarnotta captive.

What was their intention then? That he should die a natural death up there? Could that be their intention—he asked.

Yes, that was it.

"But by all that is holy, can't you silly idiots see that it's not God, in the least, who is going to kill me, it's you who will be doing it, keeping me here in this cave, dying of hunger and thirst and cold, tied up like an animal, sleeping on the ground, easing myself here on the ground like an animal."

His protest was in vain: they had placed the matter in God's hands and their prisoner might as well have been talking to the stones. They pointed out to him, however, that as for dying of starvation, it was not true; neither was it true that he would have to sleep on the ground. They had brought him up three bundles of straw for his bed and, to keep off the cold, there was an old cloak padded with cotton-wool, which belonged to one of them. And, moreover, there would be his daily bread and something to eat with it. They took it out of their own mouths and from the mouths of their wives and children to give it to him. It was bread which would cost them much toil to procure, for one of them would have to keep guard over him, taking it in turns, while the other two went out to

work. In the earthen pitcher was drinking water—
and God only knew how hard it was to find water
in that thirsty tract. As for his having to ease
himself on the floor of his cave, he could go outside
at night and do it in the open.

"What? With you watching me?"

"Do it. I won't look at you."

When he found that he could make no impres‹
sion on this stupid obduracy, he began to stamp
his feet like a child. Were they brutes, then, with
hearts of stone?

"Look here! Do you admit that you've made a
grave mistake—yes or no?"

Yes, they admitted it.

"Do you admit that you've got to pay for that
mistake?"

Yes, they would pay for it by refraining from
killing him, by waiting till God granted them his
death and by endeavouring to alleviate, to the
utmost of their power, the sufferings which they
had brought upon him.

"Very good—Oh! very good indeed! That's your
expiation—you block‹heads—for the sin you your‹
selves confess that you've committed. But what
about me? Where do I come in? What sin did I
commit? Am I, or am I not, the victim of your
mistake? Why should you make me pay the
penalty for the sin which you committed? Since I
had nothing to do with it, why should I have to

suffer in this way—for your fault? How can you attempt to justify that?"

No, they did not attempt any justification, but simply listened to him—their harsh, chalk-stained features impassive, their eyes dull and fixed. *There* was the straw—*there* was the overcoat . . . and *there* the pitcher of water . . . and the bread which they had earned with the sweat of their brows . . . and he could come outside to defecate.

They persisted in their expiation, taking it in turns to remain behind on guard over him. When keeping him company, they made him tell them about the stars and about all manner of things in town and country—what splendid harvests there were in former times when people were truly religious, and how certain diseases of plants were not known in those good old days when there was more religion. They brought him an old almanac, picked up somewhere, so that he could beguile his leisure by reading it, and stood round him watching, full of envy at his good fortune in being able to read.

"Do tell us what it means—this printed sheet with that moon and the scales and those fish and the scorpion?"

His words stimulated their curiosity and they were gluttons for further knowledge, listening to him with child-like wonder and uttering low grunts of amazement. Little by little, he came to enjoy his talks with them. In telling of so much that was new to them, it almost seemed to be new to him too, as if something alive were stirring within him, as if his soul were awakening after long years of torpor in his former distressful existence. Once his anger had subsided, he found that a new life was beginning for him and tried to adapt himself to it. As time passed, he bowed before the inevitable. Though his surroundings were strange and devoid of interest, he was no longer under the threat of a horrible end.

By this time, he reflected, he was already dead to everyone, on his distant farm overlooking the sea and in the town whose lights he could see at night. Perhaps no one had bothered to search for him after his mysterious disappearance; even if they had searched, they would not have put much energy into the task, as there was nobody keenly interested in finding him.

Since his heart had withered long years ago, what object was there now in returning to life—to that life which he had been leading? He felt that he had no real ground for complaint at his deprivations; for if he could recover his former comfort, he would recover also the terrible depression of his former life—a life that dragged its weary way through years of intolerable boredom! There was this to be said for his captivity, that although he spent his time merely lying on the ground, he did not feel the hours drag so wearily. Day followed day on that silent mountain spur, devoid of all sense and purpose, and it seemed to him as if time had ceased. In that extreme seclusion, even the consciousness of his own existence dropped away from him. He would look round at his shoulders and the chalk wall of the cave beside him, as the only things which had a real existence; or his hand, if his eyes rested on it—yes, that too was real and lived just on its own account; or it might be that rock or twig—they existed in a world of frightful isolation.

* * * * *

As the old man's anger at his unjust treatment died down, and he came gradually to the conclusion that what had befallen him was not such a disaster as had at first appeared, he began to perceive that it was indeed a very severe punishment that those three men had inflicted upon themselves— the task of keeping him there as a prisoner. Dead though he already was to everyone else, he re＊ mained alive solely for them, and they had taken on the entire burden of his support. They could have freed themselves from that burden without the slightest difficulty, since his person no longer possessed value to anyone, since nobody took any interest in him. But, on the contrary, they con＊

tinued to bear it, and carried through with resigna'
tion their self-imposed punishment. Not only
did they never complain, but they even did their
best to render their task still more arduous by the
little attentions which they lavished on him. For,
quite apart from the duty imposed by their con'
sciences, they had, all three of them, become
genuinely attached to the old man, regarding him
as their own private property in which no one else
had any claim. In some mysterious manner, they
derived a great satisfaction from this—a satisfaction
which they would miss for the rest of their lives,
when the time came to lose him.

One day, Fillico brought his wife to the cave.
She had a baby at her breast and was holding a
little girl by the hand; the child had carried up a
fine home'made cake as a gift for 'grand'dad'.

How they stared at him—the mother and
daughter. He reflected that by then he must have
been several months in captivity and present a
lamentable appearance—dirty, ragged, and with
tufts of bushy hair on his chin and cheeks. Pleased
at their visit, he received them with a friendly
smile. Perhaps it was the sight of a smile on the
emaciated face which so startled the good woman
and her daughter.

"Don't be afraid, my darling! Come here, little
one . . . that's right. See, there's a bit for you.
Yes, you eat it. So Mummy made it, did she?"

BETTER THINK TWICE ABOUT IT

"Mummy."

"That's lovely. Have you got any little brothers? . . . Three? Oh! Poor Fillico! Four children already. . . . Bring the boys up here to me. I'd like to see them. Next week, yes, that's right— only I hope there won't be any next week for me. . . ."

* * * * *

The next week duly arrived: in truth God wished the three men's expiation to last a long time, for it dragged on for over two months more.

He died on a Sunday, on a splendid evening when it was still bright as day, up on the heights. Fillico had brought his children to see old grand‚ dad and Manuzza his also. He died while he was playing with the children, behaving like a boy himself, wearing a red handkerchief over his head to cloak his bushy hair. Whilst amusing the children and laughing at his own antics, he sud‚ denly collapsed on the ground; the men rushed for‚ ward to pick him up and found him dead.

They put the children on one side and sent them and the women down from the mountain. Kneel‚ ing round the corpse, the three men burst into floods of tears, with fervent prayers for his soul and for their own salvation. Then they buried him in the cave.

During the rest of their lives, if anyone hap‚

pened to mention Guarnotta in their presence and speak of his mysterious disappearance, they would say:—

"He was a saint, that man. . . . I'm sure he was admitted straight to paradise."

CHANTS THE EPISTLE

CHANTS THE EPISTLE

"AND were you fully ordained?"
"Fully? No. Only as far as sub-deacon."
"Ah! sub-deacon. And what does the sub-deacon do?"

"He chants the Epistle, holds the book for the deacon, who chants the Gospel, looks after the vessels used at Mass, and keeps the salver wrapped in its veil during the Canon."

"Oh! So you chanted the Gospel?"

"No, Sir. The deacon chants the Gospel; the sub-deacon chants the Epistle."

"And you chanted the Epistle?"

"Yes, I, I myself—the sub-deacon."

"Chants the Epistle?"

"Chants the Epistle."

This conversation took place in the airy village square, rustling with dry leaves and alternately flooded with bright sunlight and darkened by passing cloud shadows. Old Doctor Fanti made these enquiries of Tommasino Unzio, who had just been unfrocked and dismissed from the seminary because he had lost his faith. There did

not appear to be anything to laugh at in the collo-
quy, but the old man's goat-like face assumed such
an expression that the village idlers, seated in a
circle in front of the shop of the 'Chemist to the
Hospital' found it difficult to remain serious: some
contorted their features in the effort, while others
put their hands before their mouths.

On the departure of Tommasino, pursued by a
drift of dry leaves, loud peals of laughter rang out,
and one of the party started asking another:—

"Chants the Epistle?"

to which the other answered:—

"Chants the Epistle."

It was thus that Tommasino Unzio, ex-sub-
deacon of the seminary, unfrocked for loss of
faith, obtained the nickname of 'Chants the
Epistle', which stuck to him from then on.

* * * * *

One may lose one's faith for any number of
reasons; and, as a general rule, a man who loses
his faith is convinced, at any rate at the beginning,
that he has obtained some gain in exchange for it:
if there be no other advantage, he can now do or
say certain things which he had not previously
considered compatible with his faith.

When, however, the reason of the loss is not the
violence of worldly appetites, but a thirst of the
soul which can no longer be quenched in the

sacred chalice or in the font of holy water, it becomes difficult for the person who has lost his faith to convince himself that he has gained any⁄ thing at all in exchange. At best, he may not grieve over the loss at the time, since he recognises that he had ended by losing a thing which no longer possessed any value in his eyes.

Along with his faith, Tommasino Unzio had lost everything, including the only career which his father could provide for him, thanks to a con⁄ ditional legacy from an old uncle who had been a priest. And, in addition, the father had not failed to give him a good thrashing and kicking, to keep him for several days on bread and water, and to heap upon him every kind of insult and abuse. Tommasino had stood it all with heroic endurance, waiting patiently until his father should come to realise that these were really not the most effective methods of inducing his return to his faith and his vocation.

He had been hurt not so much by the violence of the treatment as by its vulgarity, so contrary to the reason for which he had been unfrocked.

On the other hand he admitted that his cheeks, his back and his stomach should provide an outlet for his father to vent his very bitter grief, which he felt because Tommasino's life was irreparably ruined and the lad was left at home, a mere encumbrance.

BETTER THINK TWICE ABOUT IT

He meant, however, to prove to people that he had not been dismissed from the priesthood 'for hoggish conduct' as his father had been bluntly telling everyone in the village. He kept to himself and only left his room for an occasional solitary walk, either up through the chesnut woods to the Britta plateau or down along the cart-track to the valley, through the fields, as far as the little deserted chapel of Santa Maria di Loreto. He walked slowly, absorbed in meditation, and never raised his eyes to anyone's face.

Now it is often the case that when a person's spirit is subject to a fixed idea—it may be sunk in profound grief or dominated by overpowering ambition—his body, without his becoming aware of it, leaves the spirit thus absorbed and quietly begins to live on its own account, to enjoy fresh air and good food. So it was with Tommasino. While his spirit sank into an ever deeper melan- choly, worn out by despairing meditations, it seemed almost a mockery that his body should rapidly assume the well-nourished, vigorous ap- pearance of a father abbot's.

It was not Tommasino* now, but Tommasone†
'Chants the Epistle'! To judge by the look of him, one might have thought that his father's account was true. But it was known in the village what

*Little Thomas
†Big Thomas

kind of a life the poor young fellow lived—no woman could say that he had ever cast even a passing glance at her.

No longer to have any consciousness of one's existence, to become like a stone or a plant—not to remember even one's own name—merely to live, without knowing that one lived, like the animals, without affections, desires, memories or thoughts, with nothing left to give sense and value to one's own life—Ah! that was the thing! To lie on the grass, with one's hands clasped behind one's neck, gazing into the blue sky, at the dazzling white sunlit clouds—to hear the wind rushing through the chesnut woods with a voice like the sea: and, in the sighing of that wind and the rustling of the tree' tops, to feel, as from an infinite distance, the vanity of everything and the boredom and sadness of life.

Clouds and wind. . . .

The fact that Tommasino could perceive those bright forms sailing across the boundless blue void, and could recognise them as clouds, made all the difference. Could the cloud, by any chance, have consciousness of its existence? The tree and the stone knew no more about it than they knew about themselves. But he, noticing the clouds and recognising them as such, could also—why not?— think of the changes which water undergoes, how it becomes a cloud and then turns into water again.

Any wretched professor of physics could explain those changes, but how to explain the reason at the back of all such reasons?

Up in the chesnut woods, the stroke of the axe—down in the quarry, the stroke of the pick. . . .

Defacing the mountain, felling the trees, to build houses. . . . Over there, in that village on the hill-side, still more houses. . . . Toil and trouble, fatigue and worry of every sort—and why? To end by making a roof and discharging from that roof a little smoke, which is promptly dissi-pated into the emptiness of space.

Like that smoke, every thought, every memory of man. . . .

And looking out on the spacious country-side, on that immense plain, green with oaks, olives and chesnuts, sloping from the foot of Cimino down to the valley of the Tiber far below, Tom-masino felt a soft and infinite melancholy steal over him with soothing touch.

All the illusions, all the disappointments, griefs, joys, hopes and desires of human beings seemed to him vain and ephemeral, when contrasted with the sentiment exhaling from impassive things, which surpass men in their quantity and their per-manence. Human events appeared to him like cloud changes—casual happenings in the eternity of the world of nature. One had but to look across the valley of the Tiber at those lofty mountains, in the far, hazy distance, that gleamed so brightly at sunset among the glowing pink clouds. . . .

And as for man's ambition! What jubilation because man had started to fly like a bird! But just look at the way a bird flies, the simple, easy lightness accompanied by a spontaneous, joyful song. . . . Then think of the clumsy, roaring machines and of the anxiety, panic and deadly fear of the man who tries to play the bird's part. On the one side, fluttering and singing—on the other, a noisy, stinking motor, with death impend, ing. The motor goes wrong, the motor stops and—good,bye to you, little bird!

"O man," said Tommasino Unzio, as he lay stretched on the grass, "O man, stop this flying! What do you want to fly for? And when you have flown . . .?"

All at once, like a sudden squall, there passed through the village the news that Tommasino Unzio 'Chants the Epistle' had been smacked in the face and challenged to a duel by Lieutenant De Venera, Commanding Officer of the detach, ment of troops. The reason stated was that, while refusing to give any explanation of his conduct, he admitted that he had shouted 'stupid fool' at Signorina Olga Fanelli, the Lieutenant's fiancée, on the previous evening, on the cart,track leading to the chapel of Santa Maria di Loreto.

The news was received with utter surprise

mingled with amusement. People made eager en*
quiries into this detail and that, as if further
information was the only thing that could prevent
them from rejecting the story outright as too
preposterous.

"Tommasino? Challenged to a duel? He called
Signorina Fanelli a 'stupid fool'? He admits it?
He won't give any explanation? And he's accepted
the challenge?"

"Yes, of course! He had his face smacked!"

"And he's going to fight?"

"Yes, to*morrow with pistols."

"With pistols? Against Lieutenant De Venera?"

"With pistols."

Obviously it was a very serious affair. No one
doubted that he had been inspired by a violent
passion, which he had previously kept secret. Per*
haps he had shouted 'stupid fool' at her, because
she loved De Venera instead of himself. Yes, that
was clearly the reason! And, as a matter of fact,
everyone in the village considered that only a girl
who was a stupid fool could fall in love with that
highly ridiculous De Venera. But naturally he, De
Venera himself, could not think that, and hence
he had demanded an explanation.

On her side, however, Signorina Olga Fanelli
vowed and declared with tears in her eyes, that
that could not be the reason for the insult, since
she had only seen the young man two or three

times in her life; that, moreover, he had not even raised his eyes to look at her; and that never, never, not even by the most trifling indication, had he given her grounds for thinking that he cherished that violent, secret passion for her, about which everyone was talking. No, no it could not be that. Some other reason must be at the back of it. But what? After all, one doesn't call a girl a 'stupid fool' to her face, without some cause.

Everybody, in particular his father and mother, the two seconds to the duel, De Venera and the young lady herself, made strenuous efforts to ascertain the true reason for the insult; but Tommasino showed still greater determination in preventing them from doing so, being quite convinced that, if he disclosed the reason, none of them would believe him, and that it would even appear to them all as if he were trying to aggravate his refusal to explain, by an attempt at jocularity.

Who in fact would have believed that he, Tommasino Unzio, sunk in his philosophic melancholy, which was growing ever wider and deeper, had, since some time back, been overwhelmed by the most tender pity for all those little things which come to life and last but a brief space, unconscious of the reason of their existence, their only prospect decadence and death. The weaker, more delicate and less tenacious the forms which life assumed, the more profoundly was he affected by them, sometimes even to tears! In how many different ways could a thing be born—always on one occasion only and in one special form, unique, (because no two of them were ever exactly alike) and doomed to live so short a life, perhaps only a single day, and in so small a space, with all around it the unknown, enormous world, the enormous and impenetrable void of the mystery of existence. . . . A little ant was born into the world, a little fly, a blade of grass. . . . A little ant, in the world. . . . In the world, a little fly, a blade of grass. . . . The blade of grass grew up, flowered, faded, and was gone for ever. Never again, that blade! Never again. . . .

Well, for the past month or so, he had followed, day by day, the brief life-history of a blade of grass—just that—a blade of grass which grew between two grey stones brightly coloured with stripes of lichen, behind the deserted chapel of Santa Maria di Loreto.

He had followed, with an almost motherly tenderness, its slow upward growth from among the shorter blades which surrounded it and had seen it arise, timidly at first, in its quivering slenderness, above the two encrusted stones—as if it felt fear mingled with curiosity, and wanted to admire the green, boundless plain now open to its view—then up, up, ever taller, bold and jaunty, with a little reddish plume on its head like a cock's comb.

Every day, he had spent an hour or two, gazing

168

at it and living its life, quivering with it at the slightest breath of air. He hurried to the spot in trepidation on days when there was a strong wind, or when he feared he would arrive too late to protect it from a small flock of goats which used to pass behind the chapel at the same hour every day, often loitering to pluck a few tufts of grass from between the stones. Up to that day, both wind and goats had spared that blade of grass, and Tommasino's joy was ineffable when he found it there intact, with its swaggering plume held high. He caressed it and smoothed it very gently between two fingers, as if all his heart and soul were wrapped up in his care of it: when he left it at dusk, he would make it over to the guardianship of the first stars that appeared in the evening sky, so that, along with all the other stars, they should watch over it by night. And, from a distance, he would see in his mind's eye that blade of grass of his, there between the two stones, beneath the countless stars, which glittered in the black sky and kept watch over it.

That day, he had gone at his accustomed time to spend an hour with his blade of grass and was only a few paces distant from the chapel, when he saw behind it, seated on one of those two stones, Signorina Olga Fanelli, who was resting there for a few minutes before resuming her walk.

Not venturing to approach, he halted, waiting

until she should have finished her rest and leave this spot. And, in fact, the young lady rose to her feet shortly afterwards, annoyed perhaps that he appeared to be spying on her: she looked round her for a moment: then, absorbed with her thoughts, she put out her hand and picked just that very blade of grass, and put it between her teeth with its plume hanging head downwards.

Tommasino Unzio had felt his heart torn asun‑ der. He could not refrain from shouting 'stupid fool' at her, when she passed in front of him with that grass‑stem dangling from her mouth.

Now, could he confess that he had insulted the young lady for a blade of grass!

So Lieutenant De Venera had smacked his face.

Tommasino was tired of his useless life, tired of the burden of his clumsy body, tired of being treated with contempt by everyone—a contempt which would have become more bitter and persistent if, after having his face slapped, he had refused to fight. He accepted the challenge, but on con‑ dition that the terms of the duel were to be of a very deadly nature. He knew that Lieutenant De Venera was an excellent shot, as was proved every morning during target practice. The fight would therefore be with pistols, at dawn next morning, there, in the grounds where he practised shooting.

*   *   *   *   *

CHANTS THE EPISTLE

A bullet in the breast. . . . At first the wound did not appear very serious; then his condition grew worse. The bullet had pierced the lungs and high fever and delirium followed. For four days and nights he was tended with devoted, despairing care.

The Signora Unzio was a very devout woman. Therefore, when at last the doctors informed her that nothing more could be done, she begged and implored her son that at least he would, before he died, return into the grace of God. To satisfy his mother, Tommasino consented to receive a priest to whom to confess.

The priest came to the dying man's bedside and asked:—

"But why was it, my son? Why?"

And Tommasino sighed and smiled very tenderly, and, with half-closed eyes and failing voice, answered simply:—

"Father, it was for a blade of grass. . . ."

Everyone believed that he remained delirious up to the very end.

THE WET·NURSE

THE WET-NURSE

I

"AT last!" cried Signora Manfroni, snatching the letter out of the maid's hand. It was the letter from Rome that she had been waiting for so impatiently. It was the letter which her son-in-law, Ennio Mori, had promised to write, giving full details of her daughter Ersilia's recent confinement.

She hastily put on her pince-nez and began to read.

From his telegrams she knew already that the accouchement had been a difficult one, but that, after all, her daughter had not been in danger. Now, however, the letter gave her to understand that Ersilia had been really in some danger and further that they had had to call in an obstetric surgeon. Mori explained that he did not impart this information in order to distress his wife's parents, for now the affair—whether good or bad—was over and done with; but he wished to complain of her obstinacy in that, against his prudent advice, she had persisted in wearing, up to the very last moment, a tight corset and high-heeled shoes.

"High-heeled shoes! What a fool the man is!"

Signora Manfroni repeated the word "fool" testily several times during her perusal of the letter. All at once she started, more put out than ever, and raised her eyes from the paper, looking round as if in search of some one on whom to vent her annoyance.

"What! What! ! . . . Oh! so the wet-nurse mustn't be a Roman? And why not, pray, Signor Mori? The Roman wet-nurses ask too high a figure! Oh! so now we are out to economise, are we? As if Ersilia's dowry didn't enable a socialist lawyer to indulge in any such luxury. What next! A fine figure Ersilia will cut, as she drives about Rome with a wild peasant woman from Sicily sitting beside her. Who ever heard of putting that sort of girl into a wet-nurse's uniform? Why, one would have to scrub her half-a-dozen times first!

"Fool! fool! fool!"

"Hallo? Nothing to eat to-day? Why isn't the table laid yet?"

Signor Manfroni came in, uttering his usual complaint: he had already been scolding the maid and the cook, outside.

"All right, Saverio, don't get annoyed," said his wife. "You know there's always a lot of work to get through in this house."

176

"Lot of work? You people? What about me?"

"You'd better pass the time reading this fine letter from your very dear son·in·law."

"About Ersilia?"

"You'll see."

Signor Manfroni calmed down at once, read through the letter and folded it up, remarking:—

"Splendid! I've got the very wet·nurse we need!"

Signor Manfroni often had these flashes of inspiration and was the first to be dazzled by their brilliance: in his opinion it was to them that he owed the fine fortune which he had amassed in trade.

With a jeering, sceptical air Signora Manfroni enquired:—

"And who may that be?"

"Titta Marullo's wife."

"What! the wife of that gallows·bird?"

"Be quiet!"

"The wife of that mob·leader?"

"Be quiet!"

"The wife of a convict?"

"Just let me explain!" cried Manfroni. "You are a woman, and instead of putting grey matter in your skull to guide you through life, I'm afraid the Almighty put tow, my dear girl, tow! Well, in view of the rotten social conditions under which we are living . . ."

"What on earth have our social conditions got

to do with the matter?" asked his wife in great surprise.

"Of course they have to do with it!" retorted Signor Saverio Manfroni furiously. "They have a great deal to do with it, because we who have succeeded in amassing a bit of wealth by dint of our hard and—what's the word?—unremitting— no, not that . . . yes, that's the word—unremit, ting toil, we are now—please observe—up against a future which becomes day by day more uncertain and threatening. . . . Do you follow me?"

"No! What do you mean?"

"Didn't I say so? Not grey matter but tow is what you've got inside your head!"

Seizing a chair, he brought it close beside the one in which his wife was sitting and plumped himself down in it with an angry snort.

With an effort to keep his voice low, so that the servants would not overhear, he continued:—

"I turned Titta Marullo out of the bakery, you'll note, on account of his revolutionary ideas."

"They are just the same as those of Signor Mori, to whom you gave our daughter."

"Will you let me speak!" shouted Manfroni. "Why did I give him our daughter? Firstly, because Ennio is a splendid young fellow; secondly, my dear girl, because he is a socialist. The marriage fitted in well with my plans, so I sanctioned it. Do you know why I am so highly respected by all the

rabble to whom I give employment? You don't
understand! That's the worst of having tow for
brains. But Ennio has nothing to do with this case:
we were talking of Titta Marullo. I turned him
out of the bakery and the wretched fellow couldn't
find another job; so then he behaved in such a way
that he was convicted and sent off to confinement
on a penal island. Now I am one of the rich, it's
true, but nevertheless I have something beating
inside me which is called a heart; so I take his wife,
put her into a third-class carriage and despatch her
to Rome to be the wet-nurse of my grand-child!"

Signor Manfroni may have had any number of
arguments to adduce, but he also had, on one of
his cheek-bones, a most absurd mole at which his
wife would stare coldly, and even contemptuously,
whenever she found herself compelled to give way
to those arguments. When Signor Manfroni
noticed her gaze rivetted on his mole, he always
became so nervous that he was afraid he would
begin to talk nonsense, so he broke off the discussion. On this occasion he rang the bell and
gave an order to the maid:—

"Tell Lisi to come here at once."

Lisi, who worked as coachman and handy-man,
appeared at the door: he had no coat on and his
shirt-sleeves were rolled up: he opened his mouth
in a silent grin, as was his habit whenever his
employers summoned him to their presence. He

was a boy in whom Signor Manfroni had dis⁄
covered extraordinary intelligence the moment
he had first come across him.

"Do you know where Titta Marullo's wife
lives?"

"Yes, Sir. I understand," replied Lisi, raising
one of his shoulders and contorting his body, while
a fatuous grin spread all over his features.

"What do you understand, you fool?" shouted
Manfroni at him: he was not in a mood to admire
the youth just then.

Lisi wriggled again, as if he had just been paid
a handsome compliment by his master, and
answered:—

"I'll go and tell her about it, Sir."

"Tell her to come here at once. I must speak
to her."

Shortly afterwards Signor Manfroni had a strik⁄
ing proof of Lisi's unusual intelligence; for, while
he and his wife were still sitting at table, there
suddenly burst into the room a woman with a two⁄
months'⁄old babe in her arms: it was Annicchia,
Titta Marullo's wife.

"Oh! Sir, oh! kind Sir!" she cried, with tears of
joy. "Let me kiss your hand!"

She threw herself on her knees at his feet, while
the maid and the cook watched the scene from the
door⁄way, Lisi standing in front of them with a
rapturous, happy grin.

THE WET-NURSE

A lively struggle ensued between the eyes and the eyebrows of Signor Saverio Manfroni. The eyes wanted to open to their widest extent in sudden astonishment, while at the same moment the brows were drawn down by anger. He quickly withdrew the hand which the young woman was endeavouring to kiss, turned to the door-way and shouted:—

"Outside! Get out, all of you! No, Lisi, you come here! What've you been telling her?"

"That Titta is coming back!" exclaimed Annic-chia, still on her knees. "That you have had him set free, kind Sir!"

Manfroni sprang to his feet and flourished one of the chairs.

"You wait, you rascal!"

Lisi bounded away like a deer.

"Then it isn't true?" asked Annicchia miserably, addressing her question to the Signora and rising slowly to her feet. It took a great deal of explana-tion to make her understand that her husband's discharge from prison did not depend, could not by any possibility depend, on Signor Manfroni's good-will or kind offices. He pointed out to her that though he had dismissed the man from the bakery, she herself could bear witness how long-suffering he had previously shown himself, and that had been solely on her account, because as a

181

child she was brought up in his house and had been the playmate of Ersilia for so many years.

Whilst Signor Manfroni was giving these explana׳tions, the Signora was studying the young woman, picturing her dressed up as a wet׳nurse and nod׳ding her head in approval. She could already see her dressed in the fashion for wet׳nurses at Rome, with a red silk handkerchief over her fair hair, held in place by a little dagger with quivering silver flowers.

When Manfroni had explained why he had sent Lisi for her, Annicchia was surprised and perplexed.

"What about my little baby?" she said, showing him to them. "Who'll take care of him?"

She held him closely to her breast and began to weep again.

"Tata's not coming back, Luzzi! He's not com׳ing back. . . ."

Finally, raising her tear׳stained face, she turned to Signora Manfroni and added:—

"He doesn't know the baby; he's never seen this little angel of his."

"You might put him out to nurse with a small part of the money which Ersilia will give you."

"As it's for the Signorina Ersilia," Annicchia hastened to say, "you know well how gladly I would do it, but it's too far away . . . Rome!"

Signor Manfroni promptly replied that, thanks to train and steamers, there were no such things as distances nowadays; you got in and there you were—arrived!

"Yes, Sir!" said Annicchia. "Your Honour is right; but I am only a poor ignorant woman, and I should lose my way. I've never yet been a step outside the village.

"And then," she continued, "your Honour knows that I have my mother-in-law living with me. How could I leave her—the poor old woman? There are only the two of us: Titta gave her into my special care. Oh! if your Honour only knew the struggle we are having! I am hampered by having to look after the baby; and *she* is seventy years old. I wanted to put the babe out to nurse and go into service, or Titta will find nothing left of the fine home we had when we married. Of course it was only the kind of furniture the poor can buy, but it was really very good stuff, and now it has all been sold to this person and that. . . . But the old woman doesn't want me to go into service. She has her pride and she won't hear of it. Still, as it's for the Signorina Ersilia, perhaps . . . I'll tell you what I'll do—I'll talk to my mother-in-law about it."

"But I must have the answer promptly. You'd have to start to-morrow, at latest."

Annicchia still hesitated.

"I will find out and let you know, yes or no," she said at last, and went away.

BETTER THINK TWICE ABOUT IT

She lived in an alley close at hand. By this time the joyful, but entirely false, news brought by Lisi had spread among all the women in the neighbourhood. They assembled inside the single-storied cottage, crowding round the convict's aged mother, who sat all huddled together, with a black handkerchief on her head, knotted under her chin; she kept her hands on a coarse earthen warming-pan which was placed on her knees. Everyone was speaking highly of Signor Manfroni's kind heart and generosity, while the old crone, with her head sunk on her breast, uttered occasional grunts,which might well signify either approval or annoyance; her eyes wandered over the assembly with a look of dislike and suspicion. Annicchia's expression and the first words she uttered when she reached the threshold put a sudden stop to the chorus in praise of Signor Manfroni, and the old mother-in-law raised her head and looked round contemptuously at the neighbours. As soon as Manfroni's proposal was reported, she stood up, saying:—

"What did you reply to him?"

Annicchia turned an imploring look on the women, as if to say: "You make her understand that I ought to accept the offer."

"I said that I'd come and tell you, Mother," was all she answered.

"I won't hear of it! I won't hear of it!" shouted the old woman in an angry tone.

THE WET-NURSE

"I don't want to either, but . . ."—Annicchia turned again to the neighbours for help. First one and then another of them said a few words, endeavouring to persuade the old woman that her daughter-in-law should not let slip the opportunity of making a proper provision for them both and also for the baby. One woman who had come to the house with her infant in her arms and was engaged in suckling it from her capacious bosom, shouted suddenly:—

"Here! Look here! Look! I've plenty of milk for two. I'll take your baby. Just look here!"

She withdrew the teat from the child's mouth and lifting up the breast in her hand sprayed the milk in the neighbours' faces, making them stand back and crowd behind one another. They laughed as they put up their hands to protect themselves.

But the old woman would not budge: deaf to all their persuasions, she shouted at her daughter-in-law:—

"If you go, it's against my wish, and I'll put my curse upon you. Bear that in mind!"

II

ENNIO MORI, the lawyer, was at the railway station, waiting for the arrival of the
train from Naples. He was a short, high-shouldered
man, extremely thin and with a bilious complexion.
From time to time he uttered an expression of
impatience and annoyance, and rubbed his emaciated face, which was almost hidden by his bushy
black beard; then he would straighten his pince-
nez, which he found much difficulty in keeping on
his nose, or he would again and again feel the
pockets of his coat and overcoat, both of them
bulging with newspapers.

He went to a railway employee and enquired:—

"Could you tell me when the train from Naples
will be in?"

"It's forty minutes behind time."

"My God—these Italian railways! It's a rotten
business!"

He went away, looking for some place to sit
down and eventually found one, under the clock,
on a projection of the wall. All the seats were
occupied.

THE WET-NURSE

So now he had to act as courier to the wet-nurse who was due to arrive! "A rotten business!"

Though she had lived in Rome for the past two years—that is to say since her marriage—his wife seemed as if she had only just left her tribe of savages in the furthest corner of Sicily. She was quite helpless out of doors and could not even venture forth alone to make petty household purchases. The one thing she could do—and she did it from morning till night—was to scold him, in a nasty, nagging tone, and to make home-thrusts where she knew they would sting most—at his sense of logic. She also repeatedly worried him by a display of the most stupid, hateful jealousy, not out of love for him, but from mere petulance. "She feels that she isn't loved, indeed! What has she ever done to make herself loved? It looks more as if she took pleasure in making herself hated. Never a tender word, never a caress. . . . Always wrapped in suspicion—fractious, sulky, gloomy, quarrelsome. Upon my word, I did a fine day's work when I married her. A rotten business!"

And he settled his glasses on his nose, pulled out one of his many newspapers and started reading.

But even in reading the newspaper, just as in his dealings with his wife at home, he could not find a moment's solace: after almost every news item he would repeat his accustomed phrase—"A rotten business!" Still, he went on reading every day,

187

and was never satisfied unless he had gone right through the principal newspapers of Rome, Milan, Naples, Turin and Florence, of which his pockets were always full.

"They are my medicine," he used to say, "they give me bile." Rather too much, perhaps—yes, his doctor had said so too. Rather too much—but, after all, if he did not indulge in that daily course of reading, if instead he spent his time in contem/ plation of the delightful spectacle of Italian home life—in his wife's company, naturally—how much worse would that be for his liver? It was better to spend the time on newspapers. . . .

"Well, is that damned train from Naples going to arrive or is it not?"

He glanced at his watch and sprang up in per/ turbation: more than an hour had elapsed. He hurried to the platform exit. Where would that wretched woman be? She must have arrived some time ago and did not know the address of their house.

As luck would have it, he found her in the cus/ toms house, where the luggage is examined: she was sitting on her bag, weeping. The customs officials were trying to console her and advising her to go to the police station, since they had never heard of the 'avvocato moro'* of whom she spoke.

*Moorish Lawyer.

"Annicchia!"

"Oh, Sir!" exclaimed the poor girl, jumping up at the sound of his voice. She trembled and nearly fell upon his neck with joy.

"I was quite lost, Sir, quite lost! What should I have done, if your Honour had not come?"

"Why couldn't my most worthy father-in-law give you the address of my house?" exclaimed Mori. "The address—written on a scrap of paper?"

"But I don't know how to read," explained Annicchia, struggling to stifle her last sobs and wiping away her tears.

"A rotten business! You could have shown the address to a cabman instead of my having the bother of coming all the way here. Anyhow, I have come. I was inside the station. I didn't notice your train arrive. That was all."

As they took their seats in the cab, he cautioned her:—

"Not a word to my wife about this incident: there'd be the devil of a fuss over it!" And he pulled out another newspaper and resumed his reading.

Annicchia squeezed herself together, to occupy the very minimum of room in the cab. She was overcome with awe at the thought of sitting there, side by side with the master, alone with him; but this feeling did not last. She was quite dazed from her long journey, from the quantity and the variety of the impressions which had suddenly invaded her simple mind, hitherto so secluded, confined to the daily round of her narrow life. She had lost her memory, her power of thought and even of obser⸗ vation; her only feeling was one of relief that she had arrived—at last—that she had survived the fearful steamer crossing and the terrifying speed of the train. Where was she now? She tried to look out of the carriage, but her eyes hurt her. Well, she would have heaps of time to see Rome—the great city in which the Pope lived. Meanwhile she was seated alongside some one she knew, and would soon be seeing the 'Signorina' again, and would feel once more that she was in her own village— almost. She smiled at that. The images of her baby—her little boy, so far away—and of the old mother⸗in⸗law flashed across her mind, but she drove them away from an instinctive need to enjoy undisturbed that interval of solace after the pro⸗ longed, acute suffering of her journey.

"At Naples," Mori suddenly enquired, "did anyone come to take you off the steamer?"

"Oh! yes, Sir! A real gentleman! He was so kind!" Annicchia hastened to answer. "And he ordered me to give you his best respects."

"Ordered you?"

"Yes, Sir. To give you his best respects."

"He must have *requested* you to."

"Yes, your Honour; but . . . he was one of the gentry. . . ."

Ennio Mori uttered an exclamation of impa, tience and returned to his newspaper. "Medicine! Medicine!" he muttered.

"What did you say, Sir?" Annicchia ventured to ask him in a timid voice.

"Nothing: I was speaking to myself."

Annicchia felt a little puzzled; then she added:

"At Palermo too there was another real gentle, man who met me at the station and accompanied me to the steamer: he too was so kind to me."

"And did he too *order* you to pay his respects to me?"

"Yes, Sir, he too."

Mori put his newspaper down on his knees, re,settled his pince,nez and frowned as he enquired:

"Your husband?"

"Still there!" replied Annicchia with a sigh. "On the island. . . . Oh! if only your Honour, who lives at Rome, where the King is . . ."

"Keep still!" Mori suddenly interrupted her, much as if in mentioning the King the poor girl had trodden on his toes.

"If you would say just a few words, that would do it . . ." Annicchia ventured to add, in a tone of deep humility.

"It's a rotten business!" Mori burst out again; in his irritability, he crumpled up his newspaper

191

and flung it out of the window. "D'you think your husband is the only person who's been sent to the penal settlement? They send us there too!"

"The gentlefolk?" enquired Annicchia with sceptical surprise. "How could they send the gentlefolk there?"

"Be quiet!" replied Mori. The depths of her ignorance gave him an intolerable shock.

He embarked on a gloomy reflection as to the hopelessness of trying to breathe a new soul into the lower classes in Sicily, where the feeling of servility was so deeply rooted.

At last the carriage reached the *Via Sistina*, where Mori lived.

There, under the pink canopy of the huge double bed, against a background of white lace and pillows—there lay Ersilia, looking darker than ever, almost black, emaciated from her recent accouchement.

Annicchia ran up to embrace her joyously.

"Signorina! My dear Signorina! Here I am. . . . It seems like a dream! How are you? You've had a very bad time, haven't you? Oh! my dear girl, one can see that! . . . I should hardly have recognised you. . . . But it's God's will: we women are born to suffer."

"Rubbish!" objected Ersilia. "Stupid things, women! They're all like that! You enjoy repeat‹

ing that we women are born to suffer, don't you?
Can't you see what's the result of always harping
in that strain? Why! the men—the lordly creatures
—have really come to believe that we ought to be
at their beck and call, that we're made solely for
their comfort and must await their pleasure—that
they are the masters! Isn't that so? What non⸱
sense!"

Ennio Mori, at whom the hit was aimed, angrily
folded up his third newspaper and left the room
with a snort of impatience.

Annicchia was somewhat embarrassed. She
looked at her mistress and said:—

"They too, poor fellows, have many troubles . . ."

"Eat, sleep, and go out to amuse themselves—
that's all they have to do. I'd like to change
things a little. O men! Men! Blind in one eye—"

"Indeed they are, when we have only just
finished our sufferings on their behalf."

"No, all their lives! I hate the whole lot of
them!"

At that moment they heard Ennio Mori shout
out in the adjoining room:—

"The whole blasted world!"

In answer came another shout, directly after:—

"Here I am, Sir! What are your orders?"

Ersilia burst out laughing and explained to
Annicchia:—

"I have a deaf maid. As soon as one raises one's

voice, she thinks she's being called: Margherita! Margherita!"

The deaf old servant appeared at the door-way, looking offended and taken aback. In the other room Mori, his eyes starting out of his head with fury, had made her a gesture that was far from polite.

"Listen, Margherita," Ersilia continued. "This is the wet-nurse, just arrived. . . . Yes, just come. Well, now you show her her room. Do you under-stand? Go and wash," she added, turning to Annicchia, "you're black with smoke."

Annicchia put her head forward to look at herself in the mirror of the wardrobe and raised her hands crying:—

"Gracious heavens!"

What with the smuts of the railway journey and the tears shed in the station, her face was streaked with grime. Before going to wash, however, she insisted on telling her adventures to her 'Signorina', with the liveliest gesticulation and frequent exclam-ations, which made the deaf servant gape with astonishment. She related all the incidents of her travel by ship and train, telling how at one stage in her journey she had felt her breasts ready to burst with the accumulation of milk, and had begun to cry like a child. Her travelling com-panions asked what was the matter, but she was ashamed to tell them. At last they understood and

then a young man—a low fellow—suggested that
he should suck the milk; he treated it as a joke and
stretched out his hands to her breast, but she had
screamed and threatened to throw herself out of
the train. Fortunately, however, an old man seated
next to her had taken her out at the next station,
into another compartment, where there was a
woman with a three-months'-old baby—a wretched
little thing—and in the end she had been able to
get it to suck and then she had gradually recovered
from her misery.

Ersilia, who thought herself now quite a woman
of the mainland, disliked this naïve display of
rustic modesty.

"That'll do, run along and wash. You can tell
me later all about my mother and daddy. Be off
with you, now!"

"But the baby?" asked Annicchia. "Won't you
let me see him? I'll just have one look at him and
go."

"He's there," said Ersilia, pointing to the cradle,
"but you mustn't touch the curtain with your
dirty hands. Here, Margherita, show him to her."

Surrounded by a profusion of ribbons, veils and
lace, Annicchia saw a little monstrosity with a
purplish face, an even more wretched specimen
than the baby which she had suckled in the train.
She exclaimed, however:—

"What a darling! He's sleeping like an angel,

the little lamb! Your Honour will see what a fine lad I'll make of him. . . . My Luzziddu was also born just like that—ever so tiny: you should see him now!"

She stopped, nearly breaking down at the thought of him.

"I'll go and come straight back," she said, and followed the maid into the next room.

III

SHE would have liked to put the little one to her breast at once, and the master of the house agreed with her, but Ersilia, who must, of course, oppose her husband on every point, would not hear of it. No. The milk must be examined by a doctor first.

"What's the need of the doctor?" asked Annicchia with a smile. "Can't you see how well I am?"

She undoubtedly was the picture of health, fresh and rosy.

Ersilia shot an angry glance at her from the bed, suspecting that the purpose of these words had been to arouse the husband's attention.

"The doctor! I want the doctor at once!" she insisted.

Muttering his usual expletive, Mori had to go for the doctor.

By the time the doctor came—towards evening—Annicchia was again in great pain from her swollen breasts, and as they had been unable to induce the baby to suck from the mother, who anyhow had no milk to give it, it was mad with hunger.

BETTER THINK TWICE ABOUT IT

Ennio wanted to remain in the room during the doctor's visit, but his wife drove him away.

"There's nothing to see. Don't stay in here. Go and tell Margherita to bring a spoon and a glass of water."

"A blonde, eh? . . . blonde . . ." the doctor was saying. He had a way of repeating a word three or four times, with a look of great abstraction, as if he were constantly struggling against the difficulty of concentrating his mind.

When Annicchia saw him observing her with such close attention, she blushed as red as a poppy.

"A blonde, eh? Yes, I think we must call her that, my dear lady," the doctor continued, "a blonde, don't you think, dear lady? . . . a handsome young woman, too . . . handsome and healthy . . . yes, healthy as well. . . . But a brunette, eh? a brunette . . . a brunette would have been better. . . . The milk of a brunette, certainly, the milk of a brunette. . . . Well, let me have a look at her."

Making Annicchia hold her head up, he examined the glands of the neck; then after further scrutiny began abstractedly to unbutton her vest. At this Annicchia was overcome with surprise and embarrassment. Trembling with shame, she tried to stop him, covering her breasts with her hands.

"Put them out, eh? put them out!" said the doctor.

Ersilia burst out laughing.

"Why are you . . . er . . . why are you laugh-ing, my dear lady?"

Can't you see how shocked that silly creature is?" explained Ersilia.

"At me? But I am the doctor!"

"She's not used to it," continued Ersilia. "And then—you know, Doctor—we Sicilian women are not at all like the women over here."

"Ah!" rejoined the doctor. "I understand . . . understand . . . I quite see . . . quite see. . . . More modest, eh? more modest. . . . But I am the doctor; a doctor is like a confessor. Come along! Squeeze a few drops, yourself, into this spoon. How old is your baby?"

"I acquired him," replied Annicchia, looking the doctor in the face with a great effort, "two months ago."

"You acquired him? What do you mean?"

"How should I put it?"

"Gave birth to him, my lass, one doesn't acquire children, one gives birth to them . . . birth to them. What's the harm in that?"

When the doctor at last left, after examining the milk, Annicchia collapsed into a chair, as ex-hausted as if she had over-taxed her strength.

"Oh! dear Signorina! how horrible it was! I thought I should die of shame."

A moment later, hearing the infant cry, she

hastened to the cradle and put him to her breast.

"There! there! have a good drink, my fine boy, my heart's delight!"

From her bed Ersilia again shot her an angry glance. She saw the pale gold hair, which was drawn back from the centre parting and formed two rolls over the ears, an admirable frame to the delicate features; she caught a glimpse of the white, shapely bosom and said irritably:

"It would be better to change him first and then give him his meal, to send him off to sleep."

"Let him suck, the poor little chap!" cried Annicchia. "He's terribly hungry. Oh, if you could only feel how eagerly he's sucking!"

When she went a little later to the adjoining room, intended for herself and the baby, she could not stop uttering cries of wonder at the furniture and the hangings.

"*Gesu!* How grand it all is in Rome! How grand!"

She felt quite nervous at the sight of that fine, new bed, prepared for her to sleep in. It brought back to her the memory of her still greater nervousness, two years before, when she had first seen another bed, the first bed that she was to share with another person. She saw again that distant cottage, as it then was, in those days when Titta was free from the pernicious ideas which had led to his

ruin. With what ardent love he had furnished it
for his bride. . . . Alas! she saw it also as it now
was, stripped bare save for a couple of chairs and
for one bed in which she had slept with the
mother-in-law.

Now the old woman would have that double-bed
all to herself, for the baby would probably sleep at
the neighbour's house. Poor Luzziddu, such a small
child, away from home and with his mother so
far distant! She was sure that that woman would
not give him the same attention as she gave her
own child; no, Luzziddu would be put on one side
and have to wait quietly for what little was left
over—poor baby, who had hitherto had his mother
all to himself.

Annicchia began to weep, but, afraid of being
caught weeping, she soon dried her tears and tried
to console herself by the reflection that after all the
grandmother lived close by and would be on the
watch, and that in case anything happened that
harsh, domineering old woman would make her
influence felt. She was Titta's mother and was like
him in disposition. But at bottom she had a good
heart, just as Titta had. As time passed, she was
bound to see that if her daughter-in-law had dis-
obeyed her, it was because she was forced to do so
and that it was for everyone's benefit.

Annicchia would have preferred to sleep on the
floor instead of in that magnificent bed under all

those hangings; in that way she could have proved, if only to herself, that the decision she had come to was a sacrifice on her own part, and that she had thought solely of others' benefit. For the infant, the bed was the proper place, because all that wealth was lavished on his account; but for herself, she would prefer to lie on the floor like a dog. She really did not have the heart to sleep under those bed-clothes, when she thought of the straw pallets on which her Luzziddu and her mother-in-law were lying.

Her deeper feelings were hurt even more, a few days later, when the dressmaker sent the absurdly showy uniform she was to wear. Were they really for her, all those fineries—embroidered aprons, silk ribbons, silver hair-daggers? Was she to go out dressed like that, as if she were off to a fancy ball?

Ersilia, who had by this time left her bed, grew annoyed and spoke sharply to her.

"Oh, what affectation! Just what I expected. It's the custom here and you've got to dress like that, whether you like it or not."

"As your Honour orders," Annicchia hastened to reply, trying to smooth her down. "I am very sorry. I thought of what great expense your Honour is going to on my account, when I am in no way worthy of it. Your Honour is the mistress. I spoke as I did, because it seemed so strange to me—because in our country . . ."

"Now we are in Rome," said Ersilia, cutting her short. "Besides, the dress suits you admirably."

That was true—the bright red silk offered a charming contrast, setting off the fair hair and the blue of the clear, laughing eyes. Ersilia knew well that when she went out with her, she would herself show to very poor advantage, but her vanity, the pride of owning a wet-nurse so gorgeously attired, proved stronger even than her jealousy.

The first time Annicchia was taken out by her mistress was for a carriage drive. The poor girl blushed scarlet with shame, and kept her eyes lowered, fixed upon the little one lying on her lap. Ersilia noticed that everyone in the street stopped and turned to stare at her nurse.

"Look up!" she said, "hold your head up. Don't make a scene. People will think you've just been smacked!"

Annicchia did her best to raise her eyes and hold her head up, and gradually her wonder at the magnificence of the city—a sight so utterly new to her—overcame her bashfulness and she began to gaze round-eyed at whatever Ersilia pointed out to her.

"*Gesu! Gesu!*" muttered Annicchia. "How magnificent! How marvellous!"

She returned to the house after that first outing half-dazed, her legs shaking and her ears buzzing, as if she had been caught in a street riot and only escaped with the utmost difficulty. She felt that she was much more—oh, so much more!—distant from her village than she had ever imagined pos, sible—it was almost as if she had strayed into another world, which did not yet seem to her a real one.

"Gesù! Gesù!"

Meanwhile Mori was giving his wife a letter which had been delivered while she was out. It came from Sicily.

Signora Manfroni wrote to her daughter that Marullo's old mother had returned the money which she had sent her—the advance she had arranged with Annicchia to make against the first month's wages as wet-nurse. The old woman had refused even to set eyes on it and had declared that she would sooner die of hunger, or go from door to door begging a crust of bread. Meanwhile the neighbour to whom Annicchia had entrusted her infant had come to the Signora to complain about the old hag, saying that she could not get any money out of her, not even enough to provide for the child's needs. Signora Manfroni added that she had given half of the wages to *her*, making her promise to provide a bowl of soup every day for the old woman, to save her from starvation: the foster-mother was to give it in her own name, as if it were a charity from herself. Signora Manfroni advised her daughter not to send the other half of the wages, as the Marullo woman would never accept it: she concluded by saying that she deeply regretted having involved herself in this difficult position—it all came of following some one else's advice.

"Your clever advice!" burst out Ersilia, as she folded up the letter. "Are you never going to have any judgment?"

"I?" snapped Ennio. "D'you think I wrote to your worthy mother to pick out a nurse who is the daughter-in-law of a raving lunatic?"

"No, but you *would* send for a nurse from Sicily! If you hadn't had that brilliant idea, we shouldn't be in this mess now. Not that you mind, of course. You've taken quite a fancy to the pretty Sicilian. I've noticed that."

Mori opened his eyes in great surprise.

"My son's wet-nurse!"

"That's right! Shout so that they can all hear you."

"Who wouldn't shout, I'd like to know, on hearing a disgusting accusation like that. So now you're jealous of my son's wet-nurse, are you? You must be mad!"

"Mad yourself! If you only had half the sense that I have! Well, we'll drop that matter—the question is, what are we going to do with this money?"

"I hope you won't for one moment think of

explaining to her that her mother-in-law refuses it?"

"What d'you take me for? I should think not. It would upset her altogether."

Mori lost his patience and tossed his head angrily as he went away.

IV

SO now it had come to this! He must
abstain from petting, or even from looking
at his baby—and all because his wife had begun
to suspect that the nurse might interpret his
caresses and fond looks as really meant for her,
self.

One day, she had asked him bluntly, "Why
don't you take any interest in your child when he's
in my arms? Why d'you have to go and make a
fuss over him when he's with her?"

Deeply hurt by her unjust suspicion, Ennio
replied angrily:—

"But he never is with you!"

It was true that whenever she took the baby in
her arms, he would start crying and hold out his
little hands to the nurse. Perhaps Ersilia did not
hold him properly, not so much from want of
experience as because she was always afraid he
might soil the expensive peignoirs of which she
made a great display.

Although she never had any callers and rarely
left the house, she managed to spend large sums

on her dresses; yet she was constantly discontented with them, as with everything and everybody, herself included. She believed herself to be un‹ happy, and perhaps really was so; but she laid the blame for her unhappiness on other people, instead of attributing it to her own quarrelsome‹ ness, to her sour nature and lack of all charm. She was convinced that if she had met the right man, some one to love her and understand her, she would not have felt that terrible void in her own soul and in the world around her. Now she had even taken a dislike to her baby, because it showed that it preferred the nurse to her. Her days passed in idleness and boredom, and never without a fit of weeping. Her husband sometimes noticed that her eyes were red and swollen, but he always pretended not to have noticed it; as far as possible, he avoided talking to her, having come to the conclusion that there was nothing he could do or say which would lead her to take an interest in anything. She was desperately anxious to enjoy life, really, but he considered her quite incapable of doing so. She expected other people to bring happiness to her, not realising that each must make it for himself. For the rest, if she was unhappy, he was no less unhappy because he had to live with her. A fine existence, his—shut up all day long in his study! Fortunately his friends in the Socialist party would come to see him from time to time:

with them at least he could expand and engage in free discussion.

During these discussions, Signor Felicissimo Ramicelli—the elderly clerk who worked in the study—was despatched to the drawing,room. He would make a deep bow to the gentlemen of the Revolution and leave the room with much dignity; but, no sooner had he crossed the threshold and shut the door, than he would indulge in a little gleeful caper, winking and rubbing his hands together with great satisfaction; then, twisting the tips of his dyed moustache, he would cross to the entrance hall and sit on the bench there, in the hope of meeting the pretty Sicilian wet,nurse.

He had already made one attempt to enter into conversation with her.

"D'you know my christian name? It's Felicis, simo."

But Annicchia did not seem to understand and turned her back on him. Then Signor Ramicelli said to himself:—

"Felicissimo,* indeed! I wonder why?"

He had been given that superlatively fine name to bring him good luck. Much good it had done him! Why, so far he had never had enough success to justify him in feeling even in the least degree contented, let alone being able to call himself lucky. He earned a paltry eight lire a day: he

*Very lucky man.

might perhaps have made both ends meet with that sum, had it not been for one unfortunate weakness—women.

He could not help it—the girls were too much for him!

That girl Annicchia, for example; what a lus/ cious mouthful! Every time he set eyes on her he felt a funny feeling at the back of his palate. She seemed to him to be a well/behaved young woman too. *She seemed*—he insisted on that qualification— because it is well/known that wet/nurses are all girls who have gone to the bad—they're anybody's property by that time.

When Annicchia observed Signor Ramicelli's languishing glances and simian grimaces, she did not know whether to laugh at them or to take offence. The little old man, whose fair hair still remained strangely fair, seemed to her a quaint specimen. If he was not yet out of his mind, he couldn't be far off it.

One day she was in the entrance hall, engaged in trying out the baby's little legs, supporting him under the arms. She called the child 'Nonida', not having learned, during her six months' stay, how to pronounce the christian name which Signor Mori had given his son—Leonida.

"How silly you are . . . 'Nonida', indeed!" said Signor Ramicelli, to tease her. "It's Le/o/nida."

"I can't say it."

"Well, *Felicissimo*, then? Can't you say that either? That's my name, you know."

Annicchia picked up the child and left the hall, remarking:—

"I don't believe it."

"Neither do I," was Signor Ramicelli's philo-sophic conclusion, as he sat there waiting for the end of the discussion going on in the study. *Tactics. . . . Scoundrels. . . . The education of the proletariat. . . . The minimum programme. . . .* —These and similar expressions reached Signor Ramicelli's ears from time to time, but he paid no attention to them; he sighed and shook his head despondently, turning round so as to keep one eye on the door-way through which the wet-nurse had disappeared. Every now and then he caught the sound of a folk-song—a plaintive lullaby which Annicchia was softly crooning. She was thinking of her own baby, as she watched her nurseling, who by this time had grown into a fine fat child, even bigger than her own had been when she left him over there. Oh! he would have been a giant by this time, for sure—her poor Luzziddu, if she had been able to go on nursing him. As it was, who could say what might have happened? She was haunted by such terrible ideas about him. She often saw him in her dreams—sick, ghastly thin, just skin and bone, with a feeble neck and a large rickety head which flopped first on one shoulder

then on the other, whilst she stood gazing at him—
unable to stir, horror-struck. . . . Was that her
Luzziddu? In that pitiable condition? . . . In her
dream she would hasten to give him her milk, but
the child always scowled at her—with the savage
eyes of his grandmother—and turned his face
away, refusing the breast she offered. How
horrible! She would wake up with a shudder and
lie tossing about till day-break, unable to get rid
of the picture of her baby reduced to that ghastly
state.

She no longer dared to mention her anxiety to
her mistress, who had often answered her angrily,
annoyed perhaps by her too frequent enquiries, or
thinking that she was neglecting her charge through
worrying so much about her own baby. No, really,
in all conscience, that wasn't true. No one could
say that. Just look at Nonida, what a sturdy, active
little chap he had become!

Annicchia could hardly recognise in her present
mistress the 'Signorina Ersilia' of former days, so
badly did she find herself treated—worse than a
serving-maid. Yet she did all she could to satisfy
her. Now that the deaf maid, Margherita, had
left, she willingly performed any number of services
which were not part of her duties, and she tried
always to seem gay, to cheer her mistress, whose
nerves were so bad that she would go into a state of
hysterical despair over the merest trifle.

"Here I am, dear Signorina. I'll do it. . . . Don't you worry."

In return for her devotion, however, she did think that a little sympathy might have been shown her: for example, when the mail from Sicily arrived she would run to her mistress with the letters, crying excitedly:—

"Signorina! Signorina!"

"What's all the excitement about *now*? Have you drawn a prize in the lottery?"

Time and again she was frozen by that chilly reception: she would stand there waiting for her mistress to finish the letter, hoping that she would give her news about her baby, but never a word! At last, when she saw her putting the letter back into its envelope, she would ask timidly:—

"What about my Luzziddu? No news?"

"Yes, it says that he's quite well."

"And the old woman—my mother-in-law?"

"So is she."

And she had to rest satisfied with these answers. But could it possibly be that they sent her no other messages from over there? Oh! how bitterly she regretted not having learnt to write. She had naturally expected, when she left, that the separation from her home would be painful, but never that it would be like that—a real torture.

However, in a few days' time the child she was nursing would be seven months old, and at nine months he was to be weaned, so his father had decided. Patience, therefore, patience. . . . Only two months more of that agony!

With this consoling thought, she resigned herself to her ill-fortune, and had no presentiment of the calamity which was to befall her on the very day on which the child completed his seventh month— a day of double rejoicing, for Nonida had just cut his first tooth.

She heard the front-door bell and, thinking that it was the postman, went to open the door, full of pleasant anticipation. All at once—before she had time even to see whom she was admitting, she found herself lying on the floor, knocked down by a terrible blow on the head. Her husband, Titta Marullo, was standing over her, deathly white and convulsed with rage, his foot raised to stamp upon her face.

"You bitch! Where's your master?"

On hearing her cry, Signor Mori, his wife and Signor Ramicelli rushed to the spot. Titta Marullo turned on Signor Mori, took him by the coat-collar and began to swing him slowly to and fro, saying:

"My son is dead—d'you understand? Dead!" he repeated, turning towards Annicchia who had uttered a wild scream. "And now, you toff, what are you going to do about it? Are you going to pay me, or will you give me your own instead?"

"He's mad!" cried Ersilia, shaking with fright.

214

With unexpected vigour for so small a man, Signor Mori wrenched himself free and pushed Marullo violently towards the door. Pointing to it, he shouted:—

"Be off, you rascal! Get out of my house, at once!"

"You have a care!" replied Marullo. "I've nothing to lose, so you'd better look out! My mother's in the workhouse and my son's dead. So I've come here to spit in your face and take that bitch away with me. . . . Get up, at once!" he added, turning to his wife, who still lay on the floor.

At that moment, however, Signor Ramicelli, who had slipped away unnoticed, hurried back, still panting with alarm. He had with him a couple of policemen. Shaking with excitement, Signor Mori turned to them and shouted furiously:—

"Take him away! Take him away! The ruffian forced his way into my house to insult and threaten me!"

The policemen seized Marullo by the arms. He struggled to free himself, shouting: "I want my wife!" but they dragged him away. Mori followed them to the police-station, to lay a formal charge of assault.

V

NEXT day came a belated letter from Signora Manfroni, reporting the baby's death and the illness of Marullo's old mother. It contained no mention of Titta himself.

At first Mori thought that the man had escaped from the penal settlement, but he afterwards learned that he had been released. He had been granted a pardon on the recommendation of the Prefect, to whom the sick mother had sent a petition from the hospital. The police at Rome now deported the offender to Sicily, warning him that he would be sent back to the penal island if he made the slightest attempt to escape from the close surveillance to which he was declared liable for the next three years.

Terror at her husband's brutal attack and despair at her baby's death combined to throw Annicchia into a high fever and, for three days, it seemed as if she would lose her reason. Then the delirium ceased and her hallucinations passed, only to be followed by a mental torpor even more alarming than her fits of raving. She looked but she did not see; she heard what was said to her and answered 'yes' by nodding her head or even by speaking, but showed afterwards that she had not under- stood.

Her milk had dried up and the child had had to be weaned. The whole house was in commotion: Ersilia, inexperienced and very incompetent, had been kept up for two nights in succession by the baby, who cried for his nurse and would not give her a moment's peace. In addition she had to look after the house, instruct the new maid in her duties and give some attention to the sick woman. She stormed at her husband who wandered round, newspaper in hand, without any idea of helping. "What can I do?" he asked.

"What?" shouted his wife. "Why, get a move on, be of some use! Can't you see that I'm all alone, with no one to help me, and the baby on my hands? On top of all this, I can't be expected to look after the woman who's caused us all this trouble. Go out and try to find a place for her in some pauper hospital."

At this suggestion Ennio stood and stared at his wife in amazement.

"Send her to the poor-house?"

"Oh yes! You've heaps of pity, plenty of sympathy for her!" retorted Ersilia in a venomous tone. "Sympathy for her—haven't you?—but none for me, though I haven't been able to sleep, night after night, haven't even had time to brush my hair! So I'm to be everybody's servant, am I? You just wait until she's a bit better and I'll show you! Not one day longer, not one single minute shall she stay in my house!"

She had not the heart, however, to carry out the threat, when Annicchia began to show some signs of recovery. She tried to lead the conversation in that direction by mentioning that she had kept for her nurse the money which the mother-in-law had refused, but Annicchia replied:—

"What use can I make of it . . . now? This little one is all that's left to me."

She clasped Nonida tightly as she spoke. He had come back to her again, and showed as much love for her as before he was weaned. The first time the maid-servant had brought the child to her bed, she hated the thought of his coming—for her the only baby was the dead one. But it went to her heart to see how the innocent little one stretched out his hands to her in loving impatience: she hugged him close to her, as if he had been her own son, and dissolved in an endless stream of tears which brought some relief to her aching heart.

"Oh, my little boy! What do you want from me? I've no more milk, I can't give a drop to you or to anyone. Your Mummy is finished, darling. . . ."

If only she could have found out the truth about

her son, how and why he had died, whether it was for lack of food or from neglect. . . . How could she resign herself to knowing nothing, not a single detail? How could such things be—just as if one had learnt of the death of a puppy? Poor, deserted baby with no mother near, no father, no one to care for him, dying among strangers—Oh God! Oh God!

But who cared anything for her misery? Her mistress, far from caring, was angry with her because the baby's supply of milk had been sud, denly cut off when he was only seven months old. Yes, the mistress was right to be cross with her— She also was a mother and could think only of her own child. What did *she* care for the death of that other baby? She might feel annoyance but not real grief. 'But she ought at least to understand,' thought Annicchia, 'that her boy now belongs partly to me too. If she had the trouble of produc, ing him, it is I who have built him up for her: and now I have no other child.'

Ersilia was not at all sorry to have the worry of the baby taken off her hands, but she was deter, mined that he should not remain attached to the wet,nurse, who had already come to regard him as her own property. She was therefore more than ever set on dismissing the girl. Besides, what obligation had she now to retain her in her service? Annicchia was not qualified to be either a house, maid or a children's nurse. And, then too, Ersilia wanted her boy to learn to speak proper Italian, which would be impossible if he were always in the company of that woman who could only talk in the Sicilian dialect. No, no, it would not do at all. Unless, indeed, she was to keep her so that her husband could have the pleasure of looking at a pretty girl! No, her husband must dismiss her himself.

"I? Why must I do any such thing?" Mori asked her.

"Because you are the head of the household. And because I rather fancy she's got some ideas into her head—as a result naturally of the pity and sympathy you were pleased to show her on that occasion."

"I?" repeated Ennio. "Why, I've never shown her any."

"Perhaps she imagined it, then. It's all the same to me. Can't you see? She already regards this place as her own home. We shall be two mothers to the child, two mistresses of the house. Now, however much that may suit you, it doesn't suit me."

Though he knew that he could only make matters worse, Ennio tried to justify his view.

"Excuse me, but really why will you persist in seeing evil where there is none, in getting hold of these detestable ideas—without the shadow of

foundation—seeing that I am taken up with my
work and study, and have never given you ground
for doubting my faithfulness? You must have
noticed that for the sake of a quiet life—in order to
satisfy you—I have even refrained from petting
my own child. And yet you still distrust that poor
girl! D'you think she can welcome the prospect of
returning there, where she will no longer find her
son, but will find, instead, a brutal husband who
blames her for the child's death—a man of whom
she stands in terror? Since she lost her own baby,
through coming here to be wet-nurse to ours, she
thinks she's acquired a right to remain in our
house, with that other child for whom she has
sacrificed her own. Doesn't it seem to you only
fair? Doesn't it seem reasonable?"

He was repeating, without meaning to, what he
had been writing shortly before his wife had
come into his study to speak to him. His reflections
on the unhappy case of that baby, which had died
far away in Sicily, had brought to his mind a
passage in Malon's book—'*Le Socialisme Integral.*'
He felt no remorse at what had happened, but
decided to utilise the incident as a point in a
lecture he was to deliver a few days later at the
Socialist Club.

As was to be expected, Ersilia objected strongly
to his humane argument and left his study with her
mind made up to dismiss Annicchia then and there.

BETTER THINK TWICE ABOUT IT

In his exasperation, Signor Mori seized the early pages of the lecture which he had written and hurled them on the floor. A few minutes later, he heard through the closed door the loud sobs of the unhappy woman and her desperate appeal to her mistress not to send her away.

"Keep me as a servant, without any need of wages. Just give me a crust of bread. Anything left over, that would be thrown away. I'll gladly sleep on the floor. . . . But don't turn me out, for God's sake! I can't go back there, never again, never. . . . Have pity on me—I implore you in the baby's name. If you turn me out, I shall go to ruin, Signorina. I shall go to ruin, but I can't go back there. . . ."

The sobs and piteous entreaties lasted for a long while; then Signor Mori heard no further sound and concluded that Ersilia had relented and allowed the poor girl to stay on with the baby.

Shortly afterwards, Signor Felicissimo Ramicelli entered the study: he had lost his usual grave demeanour—his face was red and his beady eyes glittered.

What a wonderful victory! Signor Ramicelli all but rubbed his hands with satisfaction, and in the lawyer's presence, too! The handsome Sicilian wet-nurse, who had just been turned out by the lady of the house, was coming that very night to sleep under his roof. Ah well! Everyone knows

222

that wet-nurses are girls who have gone to the bad, anybody's property. . . . This one still played the ingenue, pretended she thought he only wanted her as a servant. Well yes, as a servant—why not?

"Signor Ramicelli!"

"At your service, Sir!"

"Please copy this out very plainly—no flour-ishes," said Signor Mori, handing him the sheets which he had already written of his lecture.

Then he went on writing:—

"Under socialism, equality between men must therefore (as Malon said) be understood to apply in two senses: firstly, that all men should be assured, as such, of the means of subsistence; and, secondly, that all men *should start* equal in the struggle for existence, so that each may develop his personality freely under equal social conditions. At the present time, however, the baby who is born *healthy and strong but poor* must succumb in competition with the baby born *sickly but rich.* . . ."

"Signor Ramicelli!"

"Sir!"

"What is the matter with you? Are you going off your head? Why are you laughing like that?"

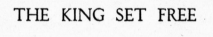

THE KING SET FREE

THE KING SET FREE

"CHUCK, chuck, chuck . . . piu, piu, piu . . . chuck, chuck, chuck. . . ."

Whenever the Mangiamariti woman had finish/ed an altercation with one of her usual abusive retorts, she started making these noises, to call her hens. The ten yellow/legged birds all ran clucking up to her. She paid no attention to them, however, but waited for the last/comer—her little black cock—an aged bird that had lost many of its feathers. She sat on her doorstep and held out her arms to him crying:—

"Darling! Mummy's love! Come, darling, come along, come along."

The cock would spring into her lap, flapping his wings and squawking, and then she stroked him down and kissed his comb, and sometimes she took hold of his flabby gill between two fingers and flapped it tenderly from side to side, repeating, as she kissed and petted him:—

"There, my fine fellow! Mother's handsome darling! Mummy's love!"

Anyone overhearing these fond endearments,

and unaware that they were addressed to a cock, might have been led to quite a false conclusion. And such a cock, too! Old and ugly, with his comb badly torn and hanging lop-sided—it would have been hard to find a poorer specimen. Yet Mangiamariti loved him with a jealous passion.

She wanted eggs from her ten hens, but was not prepared to give them food. Not only the hens, who supplied ten eggs regularly every day, but even the cock would certainly have starved to death, were it not that a number of asses and mules passed daily along that steep lane, so that the irregular pavement was always foul with dung.

Life is a chain: what some discard as digested is food for others who are hungry. The hens followed the asses and mules, disputing greedily for the droppings scattered about with careless generosity —a fine example of the economy of nature.

"How did your eggs taste yesterday, I should like to know," she would ask Donna Tuzza Michis, the only 'lady' who lived in the lane.

"As sweet as honey," was the reply, for Donna Michis never bought her eggs from Mangiamariti: "Those eggs of hers! Only fit for the dogs and I don't suppose even the dogs would touch them!"

The 'lady' wore a bright red cotton handker-chief, knotted round her head in the fashion of the women who drove the carts to market. It looked almost as if she wanted its contrast to attract attention to the skin of her face, which had the colour and the hard smoothness of a dry locust/bean. Her hands were always covered by a dirty pair of old gloves, made for a man. She had a little platform at the top of a steep flight of stairs, which ran like a ladder down into the lane. Here she would stand, holding a frying/pan in which were still frizzling the choicest rock mullet—a beautiful ruddy/gold. At other times she would take her seat high up there, before her door, and pluck a chicken very slowly and with much pre/tence of being disgusted by the task. The wind carried off the down and feathers, or the smoke and smell of frizzling, and all the while she repeated over and over again in a mournful sing/song:—

"Repent and sin no more: God's will be done: Repent and sin no more!"

She would go inside to resume the preparation of her wonderful dishes, and the delicious smells of cooking floated into all the poverty/stricken hovels along the lane. Then the neighbours would hear her singing at the very top of her voice:—

> "Bella sorte fu la mia
> Star rinchiusa alla badia . . ."*

Donna Michis' one object in all this was to make

*"A fine fate was mine
  To be shut up in a convent . . ."

the other women of the neighbourhood burst with rage and envy. Though they lived in a ghastly state of penury, beaten morning and night by their husbands and often forced to go hungry, still they had the impudence to let loose their viperish tongues against her, and to make fun of her because she was too ugly to have secured a husband.

In the early morning and at sunset, Don Filomeno Lo Cicero, the barber, went by, dancing and waving his little stick. As he passed along the lane, he sang:—

> "Chi ha capelli, che ve li cangio
> Quello che busco, me lo mangio;
> Me lo mangio, con mia moglie;
> Canchero a voi, canchero e doglie".

"Don Filome'," she said, on one of those occasions, as she took her stand in her door-way, with her hair loosened and falling down her back and her comb in her hand, "come along and cut my hair. I'm going to take the veil. As you're looking for hair, I'll sell you mine for a hundred florins, Don Filome'. That's my offer; I won't take a florin less for my hair."

"Well, I never! a hundred florins! Perhaps she thinks it'll do for a wig for the bald Queen of Spain," was the Mangiamariti's comment, and immediately she started calling loudly:—

"Chuck, chuck, chuck . . . piu, piu, piu . . . chuck, chuck, chuck."

But this time it was with a feeling of rage that she called her hens, for she—Mangiamariti—had actually, as far as hair was concerned, taken the veil. Out of sheer poverty, in other words, she had had her locks cut off and sold them to Don Filomeno who had paid her three tari* for the whole head of hair and all the live-stock it contained, whether already hatched or not.

"Wouldn't you like to buy the feathers of that cock she's got in her arms?" Donna Michis asked him.

"This cock? exclaimed Mangiamariti, springing to her feet and holding the bird on high; "why, a single one of his feathers is worth more than all your moth-eaten head of tow, devil's daughter that you are!"

Well, that year Donna Michis, for no other reason but to annoy Mangiamariti, decided to purchase a fine cock. He was a magnificent bird, but nevertheless she intended to wring his neck as soon as Christmas arrived, for she did not care to have any animals in her house, not even a cat. She exhibited him from door to door all along the lane and then put him into a narrow little court-yard, behind the house, which she called her garden. There he was to live and fatten up. As

*Old Sicilian coin, worth about 3d.

she had to keep him for some weeks, she thought it as well to give him a name, so called him 'Coco'.

"Well done, crow! That's right, crow, Coco!" she would call loudly to him, whenever he crowed, as if she thought that he was doing it to annoy the neighbours. "Eat, Coco," or "drink, Coco," she cried, when she brought him food or water; and every now and then it would be: "Come along, Coco. Come here, my handsome Coco."

The cock however seemed deaf. He ate, he drank, he crowed, when he felt the need; but as for coming when called—he would not so much as turn round. He despised that mistress of his, with her complexion like charcoal, her oval eyes and a great slit of a mouth; he despised the pet name she had given him; he despised that damp and filthy yard to which she had consigned him. He tossed his blood-red crest, flashed many-coloured rays from all his feathers, and gave a sideways look which seemed to indicate contempt. With a violent shake of his green and golden robes, he advanced majestically, planting one foot after the other with great deliberation. Before turning, he gave another sidelong glance, as if to make sure that his handsome tail feathers were not touching the brushwood in that so-called garden.

He felt himself a king and knew that he was in captivity, but he would not humble himself. Though a captive, he remained a king. He proclaimed his royal imprisonment at dawn and at all other appointed hours for crowing. After his proclamation, he would listen with an air of expectancy, as if he were waiting for the early morning sun and the cocks, who answered him from a distance, to come to his aid and set him free.

It never entered his head that a splendid cock like himself could suffer the fate of any wretched capon—that that ugly mistress of his had only bought him in order to wring his neck in a few days' time.

Before his imprisonment in that court-yard, he had lived on the plain of Ravanusa with a dozen hens at his command, each handsomer than the last, all bearing scars on their combs from the savage pecks of his imperious beak. Sweet little docile hens they were, but fiercely jealous of one another, and extravagantly proud of him, for none of the many cocks in or near that plain could compare with him either in majesty of appearance or in power of crowing.

Then, one by one, he had seen his devoted, submissive wives carried off and at last, one disastrous day, he remained a solitary widower. Then he too had been craftily caught, carried along by the legs and handed over to the woman who now kept him here. He was well fed—yes, there was no doubt about that, but what was the meaning of it all? What kind of a life was that to lead? What kind of establishment was that for him?

Day after day he waited, hoping that either the dear little hens, his former wives—now stolen away from his love and his guardianship—would be brought there to make him forget his captivity, or else that it might be ended in some other way.

Was he the sort of cock to be left without hens?

So he crowed and crowed, arousing protests from the neighbours in a chorus of indignation, rage and revengeful threats.

At last, one morning in the corner of the court-yard—what was that? Was it really possible? Yes, it was the well-known call—'Co, co, co' . . .—where could it possibly come from?—was it under-ground?—'Co, co, co. . . .' There it was again, accompanied by the sound of timid little pecks from a beak and a gentle scratching noise.

Uncertain what to make of it, he approached the spot circumspectly, stretched out his neck and spied all round, then stood there waiting. Again he perceived the noises, more distinct this time, and that call which he had not heard for many a day—the call that stirred his heart to its depths. At last he raised his foot and kicked a little to one side the brick that covered the hole left for the drainage of rain-water. When the brick had shifted, he re-mained standing there for some time, casting rapid, excited glances on every side: if anyone should

notice the displacement, he seemed ready to assert
that it was not he who had done it. Then, recover‑
ing his confidence, he stooped down and there,
inside the hole, he caught a glimpse of a pretty
little pullet with black and white stripes. First
her beak emerged through the gap; then her
whole head appeared, with its round, bright eyes
and little pink gill only beginning to swell. She
seemed to be asking prettily, with an air half‑
timid, half‑impudent, "May I come in?"

At her sudden appearance, the cock remained
quite still for a moment; then his feathers all
ruffled up as if a thrill of joy ran through him.
He stretched out his neck, spread his wings and
flapped them vigorously, uttering a loud crow:—

"Cock‑a‑doodle‑doo!"

He had called and called for so long and at last
some one had come in answer to his cry.

When she heard him crow, the pullet gave a
determined kick at the brick, pushing it aside, and
advanced, almost dragging herself along the
ground to show her respect. His breast puffed
proudly out, the cock exhibited himself to her, so
that she could admire every part of him—first the
front view, then each side in turn and finally the
back view. At last he raised one foot with an
imperious gesture and remained for some time
standing on the other; then, shaking himself ex‑
citedly, he dashed at her.

Almost noiselessly the pullet limped about as if panic-stricken, but the gurgling sounds she uttered may well have been a laugh which she was unable to suppress; for though she ran away, it was not in order to make her escape, but for the pleasure of seeing herself chased; and when she had been caught, and felt herself seized by the neck and next found his two powerful feet planted upon her back, she swelled with joy, even while held in that lowly position. She tried however to conceal her exultation and uttered a feeble, timid plaint which gradually became a clearer, rather angry cry; it seemed as if, in return, she were asking for grain to peck—indeed as if she were demanding it as her due.

Did she think there would be grain to peck for herself alone? If so, she was mistaken, for the place was full of hens! How had they come there? All of them had entered through the hole—seven, eight, nine, ten hens crowding into that court-yard, all amazed at the beauty and majesty of the cock imprisoned there—the cock whose sonorous voice they had admired for so many days past, as they scratched for their food in the lane outside.

The pullet escaped from under the king's feet, squawking a wonderful story of her alarms and adventures, and the surprise which, until then, had kept the other hens motionless became mingled with warm admiration, and they began to pay their respects, with much bowing and scraping. There was a confused chorus of compliments and congratulations which the king, with haughty dignity, received as fitting homage. He held his neck stiffly erect, as he gave repeated violent shakes to his fringed crest and gill.

At that moment, there arose from the lane a raucous crow, uttered with painful effort and broken short by anger: it came from Mangia-mariti's little old featherless black cock, deserted first by the pullet and then by all the other hens who had stealthily crept away through the entrance hole up into the court-yard.

At that angry threatening call, the fugitives, overcome by panic, fell silent. To re-assure them, however, the young king went forward to the hole, and taking his stand proudly before it, raised his foot and replied with a crow of defiance.

Expecting something terrible to happen, the hens all withdrew and stood huddled together in the far corner of the court-yard; they clucked in subdued notes, telling one another how frightened they were, perhaps saying how sorry they were that their curiosity had brought them into the court-yard.

The moment was one of anxious expectancy.

In front of the hole the cock crowed a still more haughty challenge and waited. There was no answer from the lane. Instead there were loud

237

shouts of anger from the kitchen above the yard. These cries disturbed and disconcerted the young king; they quite frightened the hens, who ran about in disorder in every direction and were so confused that they could no longer find the hole, to slip through it and make good their retreat. At last one of them hit upon it and the others followed her. When Mangiamariti and Donna Michis, abusing one another more loudly than ever, came into the court/yard, all had escaped save one, the black and white pullet.

"Where are they? Where are they?" shouted Donna Michis, her arms akimbo.

"There's one!" cried Mangiamariti, rushing upon the pullet.

"One indeed! Where are the others? How did they get in?"

"Oh! so you don't know how they got in? Don't try to play the innocent with me. Look at that! What's that?"

"The brick! Who's moved it then?" cried Donna Michis.

"I? Do you think I did it? To get my hens fed by you? No, it's you who were trying to steal my eggs."

"Your eggs! Disgusting things! I wouldn't touch them at any price."

"Wouldn't touch them? Well, I hope they'll turn to poison in your stomach, all those you've stolen from me. Look here! That brick's got to stay there, in its place, d'you hear? If not, I'll block up the hole outside. You just wait and see!''

The cock was frightened by the altercation and distressed to see the pullet hanging head downwards from the fist of her angry mistress. Of course she would never come back now, the dear little thing, after such a lesson. Neither she nor the other hens would ever venture to come in again through that hole. If only he could escape through there, instead, and go out in search of them. . . .

He decided to make the attempt. When evening came, he bent down and quietly approached the corner where the brick was. Looking up with fear and caution at the window, he gave a back kick, to move the obstacle. But that terrible woman neighbour had blocked the hole very thoroughly, imbedding the brick in the moist earth. First that had to be removed. After prolonged scratching he succeeded and at last the brick was displaced. He stopped to consider what was the next step to take.

He bent down to peep through the hole. He could just see the feeble light of the road-lamp in the steep lane outside. Suddenly a dense shadow eclipsed that glimmer and two round green motionless eyes glared at him out of the darkness of the hole. Frightened at the sight, the cock began to retreat, but instantly found himself attacked by a black devil clawing savagely at him. He crowed

239

wildly and, as luck would have it, his mistress, who seemed almost to have been waiting on guard, flung open the kitchen window with a great clatter, and the devil took to flight, climbing up the court,yard wall.

When Donna Michis went down with a lamp, a few minutes later, it would have been quite useless to try to remove from her mind the conclusion that she came to—that Mangiamariti had put her broom,handle up the hole and pushed aside the brick and then brought that cat to the hole to kill her cock. She was on the point of raising a clamour and waking up all the neighbours, so that they should come there and see for themselves the infamous treachery of that shameless wretch. On second thoughts, however, she remembered that some months before, when Mangiamariti was with child, she had been seized with the desire to taste a savoury dish that Donna Michis was cooking, the aroma of which had, as usual, spread all along the lane. The request had been refused, and, in everybody's opinion, it was the ensuing disappoint, ment which brought on a miscarriage from which Mangiamariti had nearly died. It was better, therefore, Donna Michis decided, to behave as if she had not noticed anything. She stooped down and blocked up the hole again for the night, but as she was convinced by now that the cock was no longer safe there and that that woman's malice would lead her to encompass his death somehow or other, she decided to wring his neck on the following morning. She picked him up and felt him, the cock imagining that she meant it for a caress. Then, bent on finding a safe place for him, she dropped him in the dark passage which led down from the house to the court-yard. She fastened the door, but it was in such a state of rot that it hardly hung on its hinges: it would not take long to crumble to pieces.

In his new, cold, damp, musty prison, the cock felt lost indeed. It was very dark, but little by little the shadow began to seem less dense at one point, as if the very beginning of dawn were coming there. He approached the spot which led to that light and stretched his head forward. He discovered that he had put it through the door.

So there was a hole in that door—the cat's hole: one hole out there in the little court-yard, the other here. He now had two obstacles to overcome.

He started pecking at the hole to enlarge it, and worked at it all through the night, until dawn.

When dawn came, he felt discouraged. The night's work had not been altogether fruitless, but he was in despair. With all his remaining energy he called for help.

Could it be that news of the death sentence pronounced by Donna Michis had reached the little hens in their sleep—the hens who lived out in the lane, and were so enamoured of the young captive king? Whatever the explanation, it is a fact that, when they heard his cry in the distance, one after another they slipped past the door of the hut which had been left ajar by Mangiamariti's husband when he had set out for the fields. Headed by the black and white striped pullet, they made a fierce attack upon the brick, displaced it and entered the court-yard. But where was the cock? Oh! dear heavens! there he was, trying to get through that other hole, the one in the door, and unable to manage it. They all hastened to his aid. But suddenly, the little, old, black, featherless cock dashed in among them, mad with jealousy. Blind with hate and rage, he puffed out his remaining feathers and sprang through the air as if he were trying to catch gnats on the wing. He managed to pass clear through the hole in the door and fell upon his rival.

There were no spectators of that savage duel, fought in the dark passage. None of the hens, not even the daring pullet, ventured to enter. All that they did was to start squawking as if possessed by the devil. They woke Donna Michis; they woke Mangiamariti; they woke the whole neighbour-hood. But when everyone arrived on the scene, the duel was already at an end—the little, old, black cock lay dead on the ground with his head in a pool of blood and one eye torn out.

THE KING SET FREE

Mangiamariti picked him up and began to weep over him as for a baby, whilst Donna Michis protested before all her women neighbours that she was in no way responsible, and moreover that the previous evening, to prevent any further dispute, she had shut up her cock in that passage. She pointed out that the door from the yard to the passage was still fastened. The quarrel between the two women threatened to become more bitter than the duel between their cocks. It ended in Mangiamariti's claiming Donna Michis' cock in exchange for the bird which had been killed.

"What do you expect me to do with your cock?" shouted Donna Michis.

"You can eat it," retorted Mangiamariti. "Didn't you buy the other simply to eat it? Eat this one instead and I hope it'll poison you!"

The neighbours all supported the proposed exchange, and so strong was public opinion that in the end Donna Michis had to give way.

So at last, when the sun rose, the young king regained his liberty and left the house of Donna Michis amid the applause of the gossips of the neighbourhood, escorted in triumph by the hens who had procured his freedom—a joyous company, headed by the black and white pullet.

THE CROW OF MIZZARO

THE CROW OF MIZZARO

A PARTY of shepherds on a holiday were climbing up the steep cliffs of Mizzaro, when they came upon a nest where a large crow was quietly brooding on a clutch of eggs. They captured him with shouts of amusement:—

"Hallo, daddy! What are you doing there? . . . Just look at him! Sitting on the eggs! . . . Look here, daddy, that's your wife's job, you know."

Needless to say, the crow explained his reasons, but his expostulations in the corvine tongue were unintelligible to them. The shepherds amused themselves teasing him the whole day long; then one of them took him home to his village, but the following day, not knowing what to do with him, he tied a little bronze bell to his neck and set him free, saying:—

"Be off and amuse yourself!"

*   *   *   *   *

None but the crow himself could know what impression was made on him by that noisy pendant attached to his neck which he bore high into the air; but, if one could judge from his lofty flights, he found a certain pleasure in it and had quite for‹ gotten his nest and his mate.

"Din dindin din dindin . . ."

Peasants bending low over the soil would straighten themselves up when they heard the bell and look in every direction across the immense sunlit plain. They would peer into the distance and ask each other:—

"Where are they ringing the bell?"

There was not a breath of wind; it must be very far away, that church whose joyous tinkle reached them there on the plain; which church could it possibly be?

They fancied all kinds of explanations, but never dreamt that it was a crow who was ringing the bell, high up in the sky.

"It's the spirits!" thought Ciché, who worked quite alone on a holding. He was digging pits round his almond trees, to fill them with manure. He crossed himself, for he had a devout belief in the spirits. Sometimes he would even hear his name spoken, when he was returning late in the evening from the country‹side, along the high‹ road, close to the disused brick‹kilns where, as everyone knows, the spirits have their home. He could hear them quite plainly, calling him: "Ciché! Ciché!"—just like that—and his hair would stand on end under his cap.

THE CROW OF MIZZARO

He caught the sound of that bell, first from a distance, then nearer, then farther off again: for miles around there was not a living soul—only fields and trees and plants, things which can neither speak nor hear; their impassivity increased his alarm. Later on, he went for his lunch which he had brought from home that morning and left in his wallet, hanging with his coat from the branch of an olive tree a long way off. The lunch consisted of half a loaf of bread and an onion. Lo and behold! the onion was still in the wallet, but the half loaf of bread was no longer to be found. This happened on three occasions within a few days.

He did not breathe a word to anyone, knowing that when the spirits start playing tricks on a man, woe unto him if he utters a complaint! They bide their time and torment him more seriously on the next occasion.

"I don't feel well," Ciché replied to his wife at night, when he returned home from work; she had asked why he looked so strangely.

"But you can eat all right!" his wife pointed out to him shortly afterwards, when she saw him start ravenously on his soup, pouring down one spoonful after another.

"Oh, yes! I can eat," growled Ciché, who had had no food since the morning and was enraged at being unable to confide his troubles to anyone.

At last, the news spread through the neighbourhood that it was that rascal of a crow who flew about in the sky ringing the bell.

"I take my dying, solemn oath," Ciché said, "that I'll make him pay for it!"

So the next day he took with him in his wallet four dry beans and as many lengths of string together with the half loaf of bread and the onion. When he arrived at his holding, the first thing he did was to take the saddle off his ass and turn him out to graze on the stubble that grew on the hill/side. Ciché used to talk to his ass, as the peasants often do, and the animal would prick up first one ear and then the other and give an occasional snort, as if in reply.

"Go, Ciccio, be off with you!" Ciché said to him that day. "Keep a good look/out and you'll see what fun we're going to have."

He then bored holes in the beans, passed the bits of string through the holes and fastened them to the saddle. He placed the beans on the wallet and the wallet on the ground and went off to a distance and started digging.

An hour passed, then a second hour; from time to time Ciché stopped work, thinking he heard the bell ringing in the air. He stood upright and listened intently—not a sound! So he went on digging.

Lunch time came. After hesitating whether to fetch his bread or to wait a little longer, Ciché at

last went up, but when he saw how neatly his trap
was arranged on the wallet, he decided not to spoil
it. Just at that moment he heard distinctly a distant
tinkle and raised his head.

"There he comes!"

With his heart in his mouth Ciché crept away,
bending low and moving quietly, and concealed
himself at a distance.

The crow, however, seemed to be amusing himself ringing his bell: he circled round, high over-
head, but did not alight.

"Perhaps he sees me," thought Ciché, and left
his hiding-place to find another one further off.

Still the crow continued flying high and showed
no signs of intending to come down. Ciché,
hungry though he was, would not abandon the
contest. He went on with his work again. "Wait
a bit! Wait a bit!" he said to himself. But the
crow remained high in the air, just as if he were
doing so on purpose. Ciché grew very hungry and
the thought of his bread, only a short distance away,
and yet out of his reach, goaded him to fury. His
stomach gnawed savagely, but he held on with
sullen obstinacy.

"You'll come down soon. You must be hungry
too."

All this time the crow seemed to be answering
contemptuously from the air, with his bell saying:—

"Nor you nor me! Nor you nor me!"

The whole day passed in this fashion. By the time Ciché came to re'saddle his ass—the four beans dangling from the saddle like a new sort of decoration—he was in a very bad temper and vented his annoyance on his steed. On his home' ward journey he bit angrily into the loaf which had caused him such torment during the day: with every mouthful he addressed some abusive term to the crow for not having allowed himself to be caught—"villain, thief, traitor!"

On the following day, however, success came.

He had arranged the trap with the same care and started on his work, when, soon afterwards, he heard the bell ring wildly, close at hand, accom' panied by desperate cawing and a furious fluttering of wings. Hastening to the spot, he found the crow caught, half'strangled by the string which issued from his beak.

"Oho! So it took you in, did it?" he said to the bird, catching him by the wings. "That's a good bean—that is. Now it's my turn, you foul beast. You're going to get it."

He cut the string and gave the crow a couple of blows on the head with his fist, just to start with. "That's one for scaring me and the other for keep' ing me hungry."

The ass, which had been grazing in the stubble on the slope close by, took fright at the loud cawing of the crow and began to run away, but Ciché called out to the animal and stopped him, then showed him, from a distance, the black miscreant.

"Here he is, Ciccio, d'you see? We've got him! we've got him!"

He fastened the crow by the feet to the tree and returned to his work. While he dug, he thought over the best revenge to take: he decided to clip the wings so that the bird could not fly, and then give him over to be teased by his children and the other boys of the neighbourhood. He smiled at the thought.

When evening came, he put the saddle on his ass, and strung up the crow by the legs so that he dangled from the crupper. Then he mounted and set off. When the bell on the crow's neck began to tinkle, the ass pricked his ears and jibbed.

"*Arri!*" shouted Ciché to him, giving a jerk to the halter.

The ass began to move again, but he was by no means satisfied with the unusual noise which accompanied the slow patter of his hoofs on the dusty road.

As he went on his way, Ciché reflected that from that day onwards no one would ever hear the bell of the Mizzaro crow ringing in the sky. He had the horrible bird with him there and it did not show any signs of life now.

"What are you doing? Have you gone to

sleep?" he asked, turning round and giving the crow a blow with the halter.

"CAW!"

At the harsh, unexpected sound, the ass started, with neck stretched out and ears pricked. Ciché burst out laughing.

"*Arri*, Ciccio. What are you frightened at?" he said, striking the ass's ears with the rope. A few minutes later, he repeated his question to the crow.

"Have you gone to sleep?"

He smote the crow again, harder than before. The reply was a louder:—

"CAW!"

But this time the ass plunged and bolted. In vain Ciché tried to hold it in, using all the strength of his arms and legs. Tossed about in the furious gallop, the crow gave utterance to a series of desperate caws, which made the panic-stricken ass gallop faster and faster.

"CAW! CAW!! CAW!!!"

Ciché too had begun to shout as he tugged with all his might at the halter; but the two creatures seemed maddened by the terror which they each inspired in the other, and the ass continued to gallop and to shake the crow more and more violently. For some time the noise of that wild rush sounded through the still night; then came a loud thud, followed by silence.

Next day Ciché was found at the foot of a

precipice with his bones all broken, lying underneath his ass, which was also dead—nothing but a heap of carrion, with what looked in the sunshine like a column of smoke arising from it; it was a swarm of flies.

The crow of Mizzaro showed black against the blue sky of a fine morning, as he began once more to ring out his chimes aloft, rejoicing in his freedom.

IT'S NOTHING SERIOUS

IT'S NOTHING SERIOUS

"PERAZZETTI? Well now, he's a queer one, if you like." He would say it quite seriously, in a solemn tone of voice, so that you could hardly believe he was speaking about himself. As he spoke, he gazed intently at his finger‚nails, which he always tended with meticulous care. They were very long and curved at the tips like a bird's claws.

Then all at once, apparently without rhyme or reason, he would exclaim that so and so was "a duck—a regular duck" and he would suddenly break out into a sort of quacking laugh, accom‚ panied by splashing noises in his throat, just such sounds as a duck makes.

Nearly all of his friends regarded those outbursts of strange hilarity as a most striking and obvious proof that Perazzetti was mad. When they saw him in fits of uncontrollable laughter, his eyes moist with tears, they would ask: "But what is it?"

"Oh! Nothing at all," he would reply. "I can't explain to you. It's nothing . . ."

When a person suddenly bursts out laughing and

is unwilling to state the point of the joke, other people present are apt to feel disconcerted, to suspect that they are being made fools of. The result is a certain feeling of annoyance which, in the case of those who are said to be 'highly-strung' may easily turn into a savage antipathy and a desire to get their knife into the offender.

Not being able to stick a knife into Perazzetti, those who were highly-strung—and there are so many of them nowadays—would give an angry shrug of the shoulders and say: "The fellow's a lunatic!"

If only Perazzetti could have explained to them the reason of his outburst of quacking . . . but, very often, he couldn't tell them—he really couldn't possibly explain.

The man had a very fertile and most fanciful imagination: often, the mere appearance of some person would start the quaintest train of thought, quite unintentionally on his part; the most extravagant images, indescribably comic fancies would flash across his mind; he would suddenly discover certain strange resemblances invisible to other persons, or catch a glimpse of such grotesquely absurd contrasts that he was quite unable to refrain from bursting into a fit of laughter.

He found it difficult to explain to others the sudden impression produced by these fleeting unexpected images.

IT'S NOTHING SERIOUS

Perazzetti realised well, from his personal experience, how different we all are—at bottom—from the persons we spontaneously represent ourselves as being: we may of course be quite unconscious of the deception, we may be impelled by a need to believe ourselves, or to be believed by others, to be different from what we really are; or we may be acting in imitation of others or under the pressure of necessity or of social conventions.

He had made a detailed study of that fundamental basis of the human personality. He called it 'the cave of the beast': by this term he meant the original bestial personality lurking within each of us, hidden below all the layers of consciousness which have been gradually spread over it, as we grew older and older.

"If you touch a man," Perazzetti used to say, "if you tickle him in one of the higher strata of his personality, he will respond with bows and smiles, will say 'good-morning' or 'good-evening' to you, will perhaps offer to lend you a hundred lire. But woe betide you if you stir him up deep down, in the cave of the beast. Then he will show himself to be a thief, a scoundrel or a murderer—anything. It must be admitted, however, that after these long centuries of civilisation, many men have no other occupant of their cave than a very degenerate animal—a pig, for example, which says its prayers every evening."

BETTER THINK TWICE ABOUT IT

In the restaurants, Perazzetti would study the customers, noting the way they restrained their impatience. To all outward appearance, good manners—within, the ass which objected to being kept waiting for its fodder. He found immense distraction in picturing all the different breeds of animals occupying the wild-beast caves of the men whom he knew—this one undoubtedly had an ant-eater inside, and that one a porcupine; another had a turkey, and so on.

Often, however, Perazzetti's fits of laughter were due to a cause which I may describe as being more constant in operation, and this cause really was not one which could be explained on the spot, to people in general. At most it could only be whispered in confidence into a friend's ear. On one occasion he did thus confide it to a friend whom he was particularly anxious to prevent from regarding him as mad. When imparted, I can assure you that it inevitably gave rise to a loud burst of laughter.

I cannot tell it you outright, but can only just hint at it. It is up to you to try to read between the lines, for if I gave you the explanation in plain language, it might quite possibly be considered a breach of decorum, which in reality it is not.

Perazzetti was not a man of a vulgar disposition; and, further, he maintained that he had a very high respect for humanity and for all that the race has succeeded in achieving, despite its lowly, animal origin; but Perazzetti could never manage to forget that man, though he has proved capable of creating so many beautiful things, still remains an animal which has to eat to live, and that since he eats, he is consequently compelled to render daily obedience to certain bodily functions of a private nature, which really do not add to his attractions.

When he saw a poor man, or a poor woman, behaving with modesty or humility, Perazzetti never thought of anything like this at all; but as soon as he saw women putting on sentimental airs and graces or carrying themselves haughtily, puffed up with their own opinion of themselves— then it was all up; it was a disaster. Instantaneously, irresistibly, there arose within him the thought of those private functions of the body to which such persons too must perforce render daily obedience— he would picture them in the act of doing so and burst into a fit of laughter, which seemed as if it would never end.

No man was so dignified or woman so beautiful that they could escape from that disaster in Peraz⸗ zetti's imagination. In fact, the more ethereal and ideally beautiful a woman appeared, the more imposing the deportment of a man, all the more promptly would that unfortunate picture of them arise in Perazzetti's consciousness.

Well, that being the case, just imagine his falling in love! He did fall in love, however—the unfor⸗

tunate fellow—and did so with the most lamentable facility. He no longer had any "ideas"—you understand—he ceased to be himself, the instant he fell in love. He at once became a different person altogether. He became the Perazzetti that other people wanted him to be—and not merely the semblance of the man such as was desired by the woman into whose hands he had fallen, but even of the man whom the future parents-in-law wanted him to be, or the future brothers-in-law, or perhaps even what the family friends of the fiancée would have liked.

He had been engaged—at a minimum count—at least a score of times. He gave most amusing descriptions of the different Perazzettis that he had been, each more stupid and imbecile than the other—the one when he was devoted to the mother-in-law's parrot, or took a sudden intense interest in the stars to please a sister-in-law, or in French beans for some friend of the fiancée.

When the heat of the flame which had, so to speak, brought him into a state of fusion, began to die down and he began to solidify again into his usual form and to regain his senses, he would feel dazed, quite frightened at the personality he had been made to assume, the part he had been made to play, the state of imbecility to which they had reduced him. Then he would look at the fiancée, look at the future mother-in-law, look at the future father-in-law, and those terrible explosions of laughter would begin. No, he must escape—no other course was possible—he must escape!

The trouble, however, was that they never wanted to let him escape. You see, Perazzetti was an excellent young fellow, well-to-do and of most attractive personality—what may be described as a very good match.

The dramas of his score or more of engagements, if collected in a book, as related by him, would form one of the most amusing volumes of modern times; but what for the reader would be a subject of laughter had too often, alas! been a matter of tears for poor Perazzetti—tears of rage, of anguish and despair.

On each occasion he vowed and declared to himself that he would not fall into the trap again. He tried to hit upon some heroic expedient which would prevent him from falling in love. But all such attempts were fruitless. Shortly afterwards, he invariably succumbed again—each time worse than the last.

Finally, one day the news burst like a bomb-shell among us—he had married! And he had gone so far as to marry a—no, no . . . No one would believe the story at first: Perazzetti had committed all kinds of follies, but one simply could not believe that he would go so far as to tie himself for life to a woman . . . a woman like that. . . .

"Tie himself!" When one of his numerous friends, who had come to visit him, uttered these words, Perazzetti nearly bit his head off.

"Tie myself? How tie myself? What do you mean, 'tie myself'? What fools, what imbeciles you all are! Tie myself? Who told you that? Do I seem to you to be tied? Come here . . . come into this room. That's my usual bed, isn't it? Does it look to you like a double,bed? . . . Ho there! Celes, tino! Celestino!"

Celestino was his trusted old retainer.

"Listen, Celestino, do I come to sleep here every night, alone?"

"Yes, Sir, alone."

"Every night?"

"Every night, Sir."

"Where do I take my meals?"

"In the next room, Sir."

"Whom do I eat with?"

"All alone, Sir."

"Do you serve me my meals?"

"Yes, Sir, I do."

"And am I always the same Perazzetti?"

"Just the same, Sir."

After this series of questions, Perazzetti sent the servant away, then threw out his arms in a gesture of enquiry and summed up with the words:—

"Well then . . ."

"Well then it isn't true?" asked his friend.

"Indeed it is! The truest of the true," replied Perazzetti. "Yes, I've married her, both in church and at the Registrar's. But what of that? It's nothing serious. You don't think that's serious, do you?"

"I think it's absolutely ridiculous——"

"Well then . . ." concluded Perazzetti once again. "Now you can stop laughing at me behind my back. You wanted me dead, didn't you? With my neck in a perpetual noose? Well, it's all over now, you fellows. Now I'm free for ever. I was driven to it by that last storm. It's only by a miracle I escaped alive."

The last storm to which Perazzetti alluded was his engagement to the daughter of Commendator Vico Lamanna, head of a department at the Ministry of Finance, and Perazzetti had good reason for saying that only by a miracle had he escaped alive, for he had had to fight a duel with swords against her brother, Lino Lamanna. As he was very fond of Lino and had no quarrel with him, nothing at all against him, he had chivalrously allowed himself to be run through, like a chicken on a skewer.

It really had looked as if Perazzetti's last proposal must end in matrimony—everyone would have staked heavily on the event. Signorina Nellie Lamanna was a natural, frank girl, who had been educated in England and had an English christian name. She was solidly built and wore sensible English shoes. Somehow or other, she had managed to escape from the usual disaster in Perazzetti's imagination. True, he had been unable to help uttering a few laughs, when he looked at the Commendator, who retained his pompous official manner at home and sometimes addressed him in his usual affected tone of voice, but that was all: he had confided to his fiancée a witty explanation of why he had laughed and she had laughed too. Perazzetti began to think that now that he had escaped from ship-wreck on that dangerous reef, he would be able to make the entrance to the safe harbourage of matrimony. His future mother-in-law was a pleasant old lady, simple and quiet; while Lino, who was to be his brother-in-law, seemed expressly designed to be his *alter ego* in every way.

Perazzetti and Lino Lamanna became, in fact, an inseparable couple, from the very first day of the engagement and one almost might say that Perazzetti spent his days in the company of his future brother-in-law rather than that of his fiancée; they rode, they hunted, they went to the boat-club on the Tiber, and on expeditions— always together.

Poor Perazzetti never dreamt that on this occasion the 'disaster' would befall him as a result of his excessive intimacy with his future brother-in-law, which would give scope for another trick on the part of his grotesque imagination.

There came a time, however, when he began to discover a most distressing resemblance between his fiancée and her brother.

It was at the baths at Leghorn, where he had gone, together with the Lamannas of course.

Perazzetti had often seen Lino in his under, garments, at the boat,club. Now he saw his fiancée in a bathing costume. I must add that there was something rather feminine about Lino's figure, at any rate about the hips.

The discovery of this resemblance made a terrible impression on Perazzetti. He fell into a cold sweat and began to feel an insuperable repug, nance to the idea of entering into marital relations with Nellie Lamanna, who bore such a striking likeness to her brother. Any intimacy of that kind at once appeared to him something monstrous, as it were against the order of nature, since he now saw the brother in the person of his fiancée. He writhed with distress when she made the least attempt to caress him or when she looked at him with eyes that sparkled with provocative challenge, or were soft with the promise of a sweet surrender.

At such times, Perazzetti longed to cry out to her: "For God's sake stop it! Have done with it! I can be the best of friends with Lino, because I haven't got to marry him, but I can no longer think of marrying you, because it would seem to me that I were marrying your brother."

The torture which Perazzetti endured on the occasion of this engagement exceeded by far all the sufferings of his previous ones. It ended with that sword thrust which, only by a miracle, failed to despatch him to the next world.

The moment his wound had healed, he hit upon the heroic remedy, which was to close the path of matrimony to him for ever.

"How? How? How?"—you ask—"by marry* ing?"

Certainly by marrying. By marrying Filomena, the woman with the dog. Filomena—that poor idiot girl who could be seen every evening on the streets. Her hats were like a trailing mass of green* grocery and she was accompanied by a black spaniel on a lead: the wretched animal was always in such a hurry to go somewhere—to some distant, obscure corner—that he never allowed her time to finish the numerous killing glances she bestowed on policemen and soldiers, or on any beardless youths that passed.

He married her in church and at the Registrar's office, took her off the streets, settled an allowance of twenty lire a day on her and sent her and her spaniel far away into the country.

You can well imagine that for a considerable time his friends allowed him no peace, but Perazzetti had quite regained his ease of mind—in fact he had grown so serious that he hardly seemed the same man.

"Yes," he said, looking at his finger-nails, "yes, I've married her. But it's nothing serious. As far as my nights are concerned, I sleep alone, in my own house, and as for the matter of meals—I eat alone, in my own house. I never see her, she doesn't cause me any bother. . . . You say I've given her my name. Well, yes, I have done that; but, gentlemen, I ask you, what's in a name? It's nothing serious—not a serious matter."

Serious matters, strictly speaking, did not exist for Perazzetti. He held that all depended upon the importance which one attached to matters. An absurdly small trifle, if one gave it importance, might become most serious, and, conversely, the most serious matter might become the veriest of trifles. What matter was there more serious than death? Yet it was not so for the numerous people who attached no importance to it.

"All right," said his friends, "but just wait a little. You'll soon be very sorry for what you've done."

"Nonsense!" replied Perazzetti. "Of course I shall be sorry. In fact I've already begun to feel sorry. . . ."

At this admission his friends were jubilant: "Ha! ha! You see!"

"But, you fools," retorted Perazzetti, "it is just when I shall be really sorry for my action that I shall reap the benefit of my remedy, for it will mean that I shall then have fallen in love once more, so deeply in love as to be prepared to commit the greatest of stupidities—that of taking a wife."

Chorus: "But you've already taken one."

Perazzetti: "That woman? Come, come—that's nothing serious. . . ."

For Perazzetti had married, to safeguard himself from the danger of taking a wife.

THE QUICK AND THE DEAD

THE QUICK AND THE DEAD

THE Filippa was entering the harbour of Empedocle. A small, single-masted craft, with lateen sail, she had been christened "Filippa" by the captain, Nino Mo, in memory of his first wife. The sunset was superb—one of those magnificent Mediterranean sunsets in which the boundless expanse of rippling water sparkles with a fantastic blend of lights and hues. Vivid flashes came from the windows of the many-coloured houses; the clay slopes of the plateau behind the small town of Girgenti gleamed bright in the sunshine and the heaps of sulphur dumped along the beach glittered like so many piles of gold. The only contrast came from the shadow of the ancient *Castello a Mare*, a rugged square fortress standing just opposite the pier.

As they veered to make the entrance between the two breakwaters, which stretch like protecting arms on either side of the little *Molo Vecchio* with the Harbour Master's office, the crew perceived that the whole length of the wharf, from the fort as far up as the lighthouse turret, was packed with people all shouting and waving their caps and handkerchiefs.

Neither the skipper nor any of the crew imag, ined for one moment that all that crowd had collected for the arrival of the Filippa, although it undoubtedly did look as if the shouting and the incessant, excited waving of handkerchiefs and caps were meant for them. They thought that perhaps a small flotilla of torpedo boats had been moored at the little wharf and was just on the point of leaving, and that its departure was the occasion for a friendly demonstration on the part of the inhabitants—a visit from a war,ship being a great novelty to them.

Skipper Nino Mo thought it wise to slacken canvas at once, and directly afterwards had the sail lowered altogether, while waiting for the boat which was to tow them to their berth at the wharf. Once the sail was down, the Filippa had just enough way left to glide slowly onwards, making hardly a ripple. The smooth sheet of water, sheltered by the two breakwaters, looked like a lake of mother,of,pearl. Meanwhile the crew were all agog with excitement. Agile as squirrels, they climbed the rigging to get a glimpse of what was happening—one up the shrouds, another up the mast as far as the cross,trees, and the third along the yard.

The boat which was to tow them in suddenly

came into view, propelled rapidly by its oarsmen. It was followed by a swarm of smaller craft, so full that they were in danger of sinking. Their passengers were standing up, shouting and pointing at something with frenzied gestures.

So it *was* on account of the Filippa that all this crowd had assembled! What excitement! Whatever could be the cause? Had there been a false report that their boat had gone down?

The crew stretched their necks forwards towards the boats that were coming up, but, try all they could to catch the purport of the shouting and set their minds at rest, the only word they could distinguish clearly was the name of their ship: "Filippa! Filippa!"

The sole person on board who showed no sign of curiosity was the skipper, Nino Mo. As usual, his fur cap was pulled down to his eyes and his left eye was closed. If by any chance he opened it, one noticed that it squinted. He stood there alone for a time, then took his stumpy briar pipe from his mouth, spat, passed the back of his hand across his short reddish moustache and thin goatee beard, and turning suddenly to the young sailor who was clinging to the shrouds, called to him to come down and go to the poop and ring the bell for the Angelus.

During a life-time spent at sea, the captain had always gone in humble reverence of the infinite power of the Almighty, whose decrees must under all circumstances be accepted with imperturbable resignation. Nino Mo had little toleration for men and their idle chatter.

At the sound of the ship's bell he took off his cap, exposing to view the intensely white skin of his skull, which looked as if covered with a vapoury veil of reddish hair, so sparse that it seemed no more than a shadow. He crossed him self devoutly and was beginning to recite the evening prayer when the crew rushed at him, laughing wildly, like lunatics.

"Zi' Ni'!* Zi' Ni'! la Gna† Filippa! your wife! la Gna Filippa! She's alive! She's come back!"

Utterly dumbfounded at this news, Skipper Nino Mo stood terror struck, scrutinising their faces as if to find confirmation of the fear that he must be going mad. After a moment, his look changed from stupefaction to scepticism. He pushed them roughly aside, as if they had been trying to bully him, seized hold of one of them and shook him violently, shouting: "What d'you say? What d'you say?" Raising his arms as if to ward off a threaten ing blow, he ran to the bows to be nearer to the people in the approaching boats. His appearance was the signal for a storm of cheers, together

*Zio Nino—'Zio' (uncle) is a familiar form of address used for an elderly man.
†The Signora Filippa.

with a pressing invitation conveyed by waving of arms.

He retreated, as if overcome by this confirmation of the news, and turned to the crew for help; perhaps he was actually afraid that he might throw himself into the sea and wanted them to restrain him. She was alive! Alive! How could she be? She'd returned? Where from? When? . . . Unable to utter a word, he pointed to the locker to show that he wanted the tow-rope taken out at once— yes, yes, that was what he meant. As soon as the cable was ready to pay out, he shouted "Hold on!", caught a grip of it with both hands and climbed over the side. Letting himself down in monkey fashion by his arms alone, he jumped on to the tug where the rowers were waiting with arms outstretched to catch him.

When the crew of the Filippa saw the tug go off with their skipper, they began to protest loudly, in bitter disappointment at the prospect of missing the show. With frenzied yells they implored the men in the smaller craft, which had by then approached, to pick up the rope and tow them to the wharf, but no one took any notice of their cries. All the rowing boats turned and followed the tug which carried Skipper Nino Mo, who, amidst the wildest uproar, was being furnished with details about his wife's miraculous return to life. Three years back, she had gone to Tunis to visit her mother's death₁bed and it had been universally believed that she was drowned, with all the rest of the passengers, when the little steamer was wrecked. But—quite the contrary— it was now known that she had remained alive for a day and a night in the water, kept afloat by a plank, and had then been picked up by a Russian steamer bound for America. The shock she had undergone had sent her out of her mind and, for two years and eight months, she had remained in America—a lunatic, shut up in a New York asylum. When she had recovered her reason, the Consul had arranged for her return to Italy, and she had now been back in her native town for the last three days, having come on there from Genoa.

Skipper Nino Mo seemed overwhelmed by this information, poured out upon him from every side. He stood there blinking his lids over his beady squint₁eyes; every now and then the left eye₁lid remained closed, giving the appearance of his having lost that eye, and his whole face quivered convulsively as if pricked by pins and needles.

A shout arose from one of the boats and was greeted by a chorus of ribald laughter. "Two wives, Zi' Ni', you lucky dog!" This aroused him from his stupor. He looked around him with anger and contempt at all those men—wretched earth₁worms—who always seemed to him to dis₁

appear into nothing as soon as he sailed a short
distance from the coast and had only sea and sky
around him. There they were—an enormous
crowd had collected and was lining the wharf to
watch him disembark. Noisy and impatient, they
were waiting to witness the amusing spectacle of a
man returning to land to discover that he has two
wives.

It was all the funnier for them in that the position
was one of unusual difficulty and pain for him,
since those two wives were sisters. They had been
inseparable sisters, almost more like mother and
daughter, for Filippa had mothered Rosa and, on
her marriage had taken Rosa with her to her new
home, as if she had been her daughter. When
Filippa disappeared, Rosa had continued to live in
his house. Thinking that no other woman could
be a better mother to his baby, which had been
left motherless when hardly out of long clothes, he
had taken her to wife as quite the best course to
follow. And now? Now Filippa had returned to
find that Rosa was married to him and was an
expectant mother, pregnant for the past four
months. Yes, indeed, it was a fine joke for the
mob, to see a man like that with two wives on his
hands, married to two sisters and both of them
mothers.

There they are on the wharf! There's Filippa!
Truly alive! He can see her waving encouragingly

to him with one hand, while with her other arm she clasps Rosa tightly to her breast. The poor expectant mother is weeping, overcome with shame at finding herself in the midst of that crowd, with everyone shouting, laughing, clapping and waving their caps in the air.

At the sight of that reception, Skipper Nino Mo shook with a sudden wave of anger. If only the boat would sink and remove that cruel spectacle from his eyes! He thought for one moment of springing on the rowers and forcing them to turn round and take him back to his ship, so that he could escape to some far distant place, never to return. At the same time, however, he knew that it was impossible to rebel against the cruel situa, tion, made all the more cruel by the unfeeling jesting of the crowd. Something seemed to burst in his head, his ears buzzed, his sight grew dim, he was dazed. When he came to, shortly afterwards, he found himself in the arms of the wife who had come to life again, folded closely to her bosom. A head taller than himself, she was a huge, big, boned brunette who held herself proudly and had something masculine in her voice, gestures and walk. Filippa unclasped her arms and, in front of the whole cheering crowd, pushed him forward to embrace Rosa also. The poor girl's face was deathly pale and her large limpid eyes looked like two pools of tears. At the sight of her wan, shame,

faced look, the captain felt his throat choke with
sobs. Rejecting Filippa's suggestion, he stooped
down, picked up his three-year-old child and set
off at a rapid pace shouting: "Home! home!"

The two women followed him, the whole assembly moving with them, behind, in front, on every
side, engaged in ceaseless chatter. Filippa put one
arm round Rosa, taking her under her wing, as it
were, holding her up and sheltering her from the
crowd. She managed to answer back the remarks
and vulgar witticisms made to them and occasion-
ally bent down towards her sister, shouting: "Don't
cry, you great silly! Crying's bad for you. Come,
hold yourself up and behave! What are you crying about? It is God who has sent this to us.
There's a remedy for every ill. Come, hold yourself up. Every ill has its remedy. God will help
us."

She shouted out this belief to the crowd too and
added, turning to this person or that: "Don't be
afraid, there's not going to be any scandal or
quarrelling or envy or jealousy. It will be as God
may decide. We are God-fearing folk."

By the time they reached the *Castello* the sunset
glory was over and the sky had changed from
purple to a tone of smoky blue. Many of the
crowd now left them and went up the main street
of the village, where the lamps were already lit.
A still larger number, however, decided to accom-

pany them all the way to their house behind the *Castello*, in the *Balate*, a street which eventually turns back towards the sea and has a few sailors' cottages further along it on another beach facing a bay of stagnant water. Arrived at last, they all came to a halt opposite Skipper Nino Mo's door, way, waiting to see what the three would decide to do—as if the problem were one which could be settled out of hand, quite casually!

The cottage was a single-storied one, lighted only by the front door. The large crowd of onlookers standing closely packed before the entrance deep, ened the shadowy gloom within. The skipper and Rosa felt as if they could scarcely breathe, but neither of them ventured to raise a protest: to them the burden caused by that crowd of busybodies seemed but an outward visible sign of the burden weighing upon their own souls, and hence was one which they could not see their way to remove. Filippa, however, thought differently. Lighting the lamp and placing it on the supper table in the centre of the room, she went to the door and shouted:—

"Well, gentlemen, what do you want now? You've had your look and had your laugh, isn't that enough? Now leave us to attend to our own affairs. Haven't you got houses of your own to go to?"

At this protest the idlers withdrew from the

door,way, after a farewell volley of witticisms, and
dispersed in different directions. A good few, how,
ever, remained on the darkening beach, spying
from a distance.

The public curiosity had been roused to an
unusual degree by the fact that both Skipper Nino
Mo and the two sisters were known throughout the
village to be punctiliously respectable, God,fearing
persons, who would not dream of doing anything
improper. They gave a proof of their propriety on
that occasion, for they left the cottage door wide
open all night long. In front was the dismal
stagnant beach with dark reefs running out here
and there, eaten into by the tides and surrounded
by thick, foul,smelling water, almost oily in
appearance. Among the tumbled mass of rocks—
some standing erect, others lying scattered about,
all of them slimy and covered with sea,weed—an
occasional wave would find its way, breaking,
rebounding or in places sucked straightway into
some cavern with a loud gurgle and swish. Every,
where was darkness save for the broad beam of
yellow light from the cottage lamp. Now one, now
another of the men who had stayed to gratify their
curiosity, passed in front of the door and cast a
rapid side,glance at the interior of the house.
What they saw was, first of all, the three occupants
and the child seated at the table, taking their
supper; and later, when the meal had been cleared

away, the two women kneeling on the floor bent
over their chairs, and Skipper Nino Mo joining
them in reciting the evening prayer, while he sat
with his elbow on the corner of the table and
rested his forehead on his clenched fist. Later still,
they saw that the little one—the child by the first
wife—had been put to sleep in the double-bed at
the back of the room, while the second wife—the
one who was pregnant—remained sitting at the foot
of the bed, her eyes closed, her head leaning against
the mattress. She had not taken off her clothes.
The other two—Skipper Nino Mo and the 'gna'
Filippa—were talking to one another in low tones,
quite amicably, from opposite ends of the table.
Eventually, late at night, these two came and sat at
the door-way and looked out into the star-light,
continuing their conversation in a subdued whisper,
which harmonised with the slow, gentle ripple of
the water against the beach.

Next day, without confiding their plans to anyone, Skipper Nino Mo and the 'gna' Filippa went
off in search of a room to let. They found one,
almost at the end of the village, on the road leading
to the cemetery; it stood on the breezy edge of the
plateau, overlooking the sea, with the open country
at its back. They had a small bed, a table and a
couple of chairs carried across and, when evening
came, escorted the second wife and the child there.
The door was promptly closed behind them, and

THE QUICK AND THE DEAD

Skipper Nino Mo and Filippa returned to the house in the *Balate*, walking side by side in silence.

Then there arose throughout the whole village a chorus of commiseration for the poor girl who had been sacrificed in this manner, put on one side, hastily evicted, abandoned, and in her condition, too!

Just think of it—in her present condition! How heartless! What fault was it of hers, poor girl? Oh yes, it was all very well to say that that was the law . . . but what manner of law was that? Turkish law indeed! No, no, by God! it wasn't fair, it wasn't fair at all.

Skipper Nino Mo, looking gloomier than ever, went on the following day to attend to the loading of his ship's next cargo for its impending departure. Person after person accosted him to show him how bitterly his conduct was resented by the whole village. He did not even stop or turn round, however, but went on with his work, his stumpy briar pipe between his teeth and his fur cap pulled down over his eyes, one of which was closed and the other open. He cut short all enquiries and complaints by snapping out:—

"Let me alone! It's my business!"

He gave no greater satisfaction to those whom he called 'principals', that is to say the merchants, shop-keepers and brokers. With them, however, he was less abrupt and gruff:—

"Let every man obey his own conscience, Sir," he would answer. "These are family matters, which don't concern anybody else, save God alone."

Two days later he set sail again, but not even to the crew of his ship was he more communicative.

During his absence from the village, the sisters recommenced living together at the house in the *Balate*. They shared the household work and the care of the child and seemed deeply attached to each other and entirely resigned to their position. When their neighbours or any inquisitive persons came to question them on the matter, they merely smiled, raised their arms with a look of sad help‹ lessness and turned their eyes towards the sky, saying: "It is God's will, my dear."

When next the ship was due to arrive, they both went down to the harbour, holding the baby by the hands. Only a few people had been impelled by curiosity to be present on the wharf. Skipper Nino Mo leapt ashore, held out a hand to each of his wives, without saying anything, stooped down to kiss the child, picked him up and started off as on the previous occasion, followed by the two women. But this time, when they arrived at the door‹way of the house on the *Balate*, it was the second wife— Rosa—who stayed with Skipper Nino Mo, whilst Filippa and the baby went quietly off to the room on the cemetery road.

THE QUICK AND THE DEAD

There had been universal sympathy for the second wife—poor victim—but, curiously enough, now that it was seen that neither of the women was to be discarded in favour of the other, the village became equally indignant and was full of deep resentment against that amicable solution, so simple and reasonable. They proclaimed that such behaviour was scandalous. At first, it is true, this new and quite unexpected development was regarded as a laughing matter, but it did not take long before this attitude changed to one of indignant hostility. People had to admit in their hearts—and they did not like having to admit it—that there had been no deception or wrong-doing on either side, and that therefore there was no good reason why either wife should be condemned or be sacrificed to the other; that both were wives in the sight of God and according to the law, and that hence the decision taken by the unfortunate trio was the best that they could take. But what aroused most criticism was the fact that the compact had been made in such a friendly spirit, that those two pious women had resigned themselves to their lot without a shadow of envy or jealousy arising between them. It was easy to understand that Rosa would not feel jealous of her elder sister, to whom she owed everything, and whose husband she had taken away—quite unknowingly, to be sure. At the most, it was Filippa who might feel jealous of her young sister, but even this was unlikely, since she must realise that Rosa had acted without guile and thus was blameless. So each of the women regarded the sanctity of her marriage vows as inviolable, and felt devotion towards the man who toiled for her and who was the father of her child. He was almost always away and spent only two or three days a month at home. Well, since God had permitted the first wife to return alive, since He had wished this situation to arise, they would each in turn, amicably and quite free from jealousy, await their man, when he returned for a rest after his weeks at sea.

These were all good reasons, decent and friendly, but it was just because they were such good, decent and friendly ones that people took exception to them.

The day after his second return, Skipper Nino Mo was summoned to the police court to receive a severe warning from the Magistrate that bigamy was not permitted by law. Shortly before, Skipper Nino Mo had had a talk with a lawyer: he appeared before the Magistrate with his customary grave demeanour, unruffled and firm, and replied that in his case one could not speak of bigamy, because his first wife was still entered in the records as dead and would continue to be so recorded: hence, under the law, he had only one wife—his second one. "But, Sir," he concluded, "above the laws of men stands the law of God, which I have always followed obediently."

Difficulty arose in the Registrar's office, where Skipper Nino Mo appeared from now onwards, regularly every five months, to report the birth of a child—"This one's from the dead wife" . . . he would say, or alternately, "This is from the live one."

On the first occasion the report concerned the child which Rosa was already carrying at the time of Filippa's return; no. steps had been taken to cancel the certificate of the first wife's death and hence when that child came, it could naturally be recorded as legitimate. But a problem arose as to how to register the next baby, born five months later, its mother being Filippa, whose name was still entered in the register of deaths. Either the first child, born of the putative marriage, was illegitimate, or the second one must be—there was no other possibility.

Skipper Nino Mo put his hand to the back of his head and pushed his cap forward on to his nose. After a prolonged scratch, he said to the Registrar of births and deaths:—

"Excuse my asking, but couldn't you register this child as a legitimate one by my *second* wife?"

The official looked at him in great astonishment. "By your second wife? What are you thinking of?

If she gave birth to one five months ago, how on earth——"

"You're right, you're right" . . . said Skipper Nino Mo, scratching his head again. "Then what's the solution of the difficulty?"

"What's the solution?" stormed the official. "You ask *me* what the solution is! Why, what do you think you are? A sultan? A pasha? A bey? Good heavens, man, why can't you have more common sense and not come here messing up my records."

Skipper Nino Mo took a step back and pointed at himself, placing both fore-fingers on his breast:—

"I!" he exclaimed. "What have I to do with the matter, if God permits it so?"

On hearing God mentioned, the official lost his temper.

"God. . . . God. . . . Always God. Some one dies—it's from God! Some one escapes from death —it's through God! A child is born—it's from God! You live with two wives—it's from God! Drop all this God business and go to the devil! Don't come here to report your children's births oftener than once every nine months, d'you hear? Show that much respect for decency and you can get round the law, for I'll record them all as legitimate, one after another!"

Skipper Nino Mo listened with impassive face to this outburst, then said:—

THE QUICK AND THE DEAD

"It does not depend upon myself. You must do as you think best. I have performed my duty. I kiss your hands."

And he returned to the Registrar punctually every five months to perform his duty, strong in the conviction that God's commands were being fulfilled.

BLACK HORSES

BLACK HORSES

N<small>O</small> sooner had the head-groom left, cursing even louder than usual, than Fofo turned to the new arrival—his stable companion, Nero—and remarked with a sigh:—

"I've got the hang of it! Velvets, tassels and plumes. You're starting well, old fellow. To-day's a first-class job."

Nero turned his head away. Being a well-bred horse, he did not snort, but he had no wish to become too intimate with that Fofo.

He had come there from a princely stable—a stable where one saw one's reflection in the polished walls, where the stalls were separated by leather-padded partitions, and each had a hay-rack made of beech-wood, rings of gun-metal, and posts with bright shining nobs on top of them.

But alas! the young prince was mad on those noisy carriages, foul things which belch out smoke behind and run along of themselves. Three times he had nearly broken his neck in one of them. The old princess—the dear lady—would never have anything to do with those devil-carriages;

but, as soon as she was struck down by paralysis, the prince had hastened to dispose of both Nero and Corbino—the last remnants of the stable, hitherto retained to take the mother out for a quiet drive in her landau.

Poor Corbino! Who could tell where he had gone to end his days, after long years of dignified service?

Giuseppe, the good old coachman, had promised them that when he went with the other faithful old retainers to kiss the hand of the princess—now restricted permanently to her arm-chair—he would intercede for them. But it was of no avail: from the way the old man had stroked their necks and flanks, on his return soon afterwards, they both understood at once that all hope was lost, that their fate was settled—they were to be sold.

And so it had come about and Nero did not yet grasp what kind of a place he had found. Bad? —no, one couldn't say that it was really bad. Of course, it was not like the princess' stable. Yet this stable also was a good one. It had more than a score of horses, all black and all rather old, but fine-looking animals, dignified and quite sedate— for that matter, rather too sedate.

Nero doubted whether his companions had any clear idea as to the work on which they were engaged. They seemed to be constantly pondering over it without ever being able to come to any

298

conclusion: the slow swish of their bushy tails, with an occasional scraping of hoofs showed clearly that they were engaged in thinking deeply over something.

Fofo was the only one who was certain—a good deal too certain—that he knew all about it.

A common, presumptuous animal!

Once a regimental charger, cast out after three years' service, because—according to his own story —a brute of a cavalry-man from the Abruzzi had broken his wind, he spent his whole time talking and gossipping. Nero, who was still very sad at the parting from his old friend Corbino, could not stand his new acquaintance, whose confiden-tial manner and habit of making nasty remarks about his stable companions jarred upon him hor-ribly.

Heavens! what a tongue he had! Not one of the twenty escaped from it—there was always some fault to find.

"Look at his tail, do look! Fancy calling that a tail! And what a way to swish it! He thinks that's very dashing, you know. I don't mind betting he's been a doctor's horse.

"And just look over there at that Calabrian nag. D'you see how gracefully he pricks up his pig's ears . . . look at his fine mane and his chin! He's a showy beast, too, don't you think?

"Every now and then he forgets that he's a

gelding and wants to make love to that mare over there, three stalls to the right—d'you see her?—the one whose face looks so old, who's low in the fore-quarters and has her belly on the ground.

"Is she a mare, that thing? She's a cow, I assure you. If you could only see how she moves—regular riding-school style! You'd think she was walking on hot cinders, the way she puts her hoofs down. And a mouth as hard as iron, my dear fellow!"

* * * * *

In vain did Nero intimate to Fofo in every possible manner that he did not wish to listen to him. Fofo overwhelmed him with incessant chatter.

"D'you know where we are? We're with a firm of carriers. There are many different sorts of carriers—ours are called undertakers.

"Do you know what it means to be an under-taker's horse? It means that your job is to pull a strange-looking black carriage that has four pillars supporting the roof and is all decked out grand with gilding and a curtain and fringes—in fact a handsome carriage *de luxe*. But it's sheer waste—you'd hardly believe it—sheer waste, 'cause no one ever comes and sits inside it.

"There's only the coachman on the box, looking as solemn as can be.

"And we go slowly, always at a walk. No risk of your ever getting into a muck of sweat and having to be rubbed down on your return, nor of the coachman giving you a cut of the whip or anything else to hurry you up.

"But slowly . . . slowly . . . slowly . . .

"And the place we go to—our destination—we always seem to be there in time.

"You know the carriage I described to you. Well, I've noticed, by the way, that human beings seem to look upon it as an object of peculiar reverence.

"As I told you before, no one ever dares to sit inside it, and, as soon as people see it stop in front of a house, they all stand still and stare at it with long faces, looking quite frightened; and they all surround it, holding lighted candles, and, as soon as it starts again, they follow after it, walking very quietly.

"Quite often, too, there's a band playing in front of us—a band, my dear fellow, which plays a particular kind of music that makes you feel all funny in your bowels.

"Now you mark my words! You've got a nasty habit of shaking your head and snorting. Well, you'll have to drop those tricks. If you snort for nothing at all, what d'you think you'll be doing when you have to listen to that music?

"Ours is a soft enough job, I don't deny; but it does call for composure and solemnity. No snorting or jerking your head up and down! The very most we're allowed is to swish our tails, quite, quite gently, because the carriage we pull—I tell you once again—is highly venerated. You'll notice that all the men take off their hats when they see us pass.

"D'you know how I discovered that we're working for a firm of carriers? It was this way:—

"About two years ago, I was standing harnessed to one of our canopied carriages, in front of the big gateway leading to the building which is our regular goal.

"You'll see it, that big gateway. Behind the railings are any number of dark trees growing up to a sharp point: they're planted in two rows, forming a long straight avenue. Here and there, between them, there are some fine, green meadows full of good, luscious grass; but that's all sheer waste, too, for one's not allowed to eat it. Woe betide you if you put your lips to it.

"Well—as I was saying—I was standing there, when an old pal of mine from the regimental days came up to me. The poor fellow had come down in the world terribly and was reduced to drawing a waggon—one of those long, low ones, without any springs.

"He said to me:—

"'Hallo, Fofo! D'you see the state I'm in? I'm quite done for!'

"'What work are you on?' I asked.

" 'Transporting boxes!' he replied.—'All day long, from a carrier's office to the custom house.'

" 'Boxes?' I said. 'What kind of boxes?'

" 'Heavy!' he answered. 'Frightfully heavy!— full of merchandise to be forwarded.'

"Then the light dawned on me, for I may as well tell you that we also transport a kind of very long box. They put it inside our carriage from the back, as gently as can be; while that's being done, with tremendous care, the people standing round all take off their hats and watch, with a sort of frightened look. Why they do that I really can't say, but it's obvious that, as our business also is to take boxes, we must be working for a carrier, don't you think so?

"What the devil can be in those boxes? They're heavy—you can't think how heavy they are. Luckily we only convey one at a time.

"We're carriers employed for the transport of goods, that's certain; but what goods I don't know. They seem to be very valuable, because the trans⸝ port's always carried out with much pomp and accompanied by a number of persons.

"At a certain point we usually, but not always, stop in front of a splendid edifice, which may perhaps be the custom house for our line of transport. This building has a great door⸝way. Out of this door⸝way there come men dressed in black gowns, with shirts worn outside them—I

303

suppose they're the customs officials. The box is removed from the carriage, all heads being bared again; then those men mark on the box the permit to proceed with it.

"Where all these valuable goods that we trans‹ port go to, I really don't know. I must admit that's something I don't understand. But I'm not at all sure that the human beings know much about that —so I console myself with that thought.

"Indeed the magnificence of the boxes and the solemnity of the ceremony might lead one to suppose that men must know something about this transport business of theirs. But I notice that they're often filled with doubt and fear; and from the long dealings I've had with them for many years, I have come to this conclusion—that human beings do many things, my dear chap, without having any idea at all why they are doing them!"

* * * * *

That morning, as Fofo had already guessed from the head‹groom's curses, the preparations included velvets, tassels, and plumes, and four horses to the carriage—evidently a first‹class affair.

"You see! What did I tell you?"

Nero found himself harnessed to the shaft, with Fofo as his partner. To his annoyance there was no escape from his companion's ceaseless explanations.

Fofo was also annoyed that morning, on account

of the unfairness of the head-groom, who, when arranging a four-in-hand, always took him as a wheeler, never as one of the leaders.

"The dirty dog! You can see for yourself that pair in front of us is only for show. What are they pulling? Nothing at all! We go so slowly that all the pull falls upon us wheelers. The other pair are merely out for a pleasant walk, to stretch their legs, dressed up to the nines. . . . And just look at the kind of animals that are given the preference over me, and I've got to put up with it! D'you recognise them?"

They were the two black horses whom Fofo had described as the doctor's horse and the Calabrian nag.

"That foul Calabrian beast! I'm glad he's in front of you, not of me. You'll get a whiff from him, my dear fellow! You'll soon find that it isn't only in the ears that he's like a pig. Won't you just be grateful to the head-groom for making a pet of him and giving him double rations! . . . If you want to get on in this line of work, don't start snorting. . . . Hallo! You're beginning it already. Keep your head still. Look here, old chap, if you go on like that, you'll find the reins jerked so hard that your mouth will bleed, I assure you. Because to-day we're going to have speeches, you know. . . . You'll see what a cheery show it's going to be—one speech, two speeches—three speeches. . . . I've

even had one first-class affair which had five
speeches! It was enough to drive one mad—having
to stand still for three hours on end, decked out
with all this finery so that one could hardly
breathe—one's legs shackled, tail imprisoned and
ears in two sheaths. . . . A jolly time, with the
flies biting one under the tail! You want to know
what speeches are? Oh, just rot! To tell you the
truth I haven't got the hang of it, not altogether.
. . . These first-class shows must be cases where
there's a lot of complication about the transport.
Perhaps they have to make those speeches to give
the necessary explanations. One isn't enough, so
they make a second one. Two aren't enough, so
they make a third. They may even run to five, as
I told you before. There have been times when
I've gone so far as to start kicking to right and left
and finished by rolling on the ground like a
lunatic. . . . Perhaps it'll be the same to-day. . . .
It's a swagger affair, I tell you! Have you seen the
coachman—doesn't he look grand? There come
the servants and the candle-sticks. . . . I say, are
you apt to shy?"

"I don't understand."

"Don't you? I mean do you take fright easily?
Because, you see, in a short time they'll be shoving
their lighted candles almost under your nose. . . .
Steady! oh, steady! What's come over you? There,
you see, you've had a jerk at your mouth. . . . Did

it hurt? Well, you'll get many more like it to day, I warn you, if . . . What are you up to? What's the matter? Have you gone mad? Don't stretch your neck out like that! (What a funny old chap he is!—does he fancy he's swimming? Or is he starting a game of *mora*?) Stand still, I say! . . . There! You've had some more jerks with the reins. . . . Here, stop it! You're making him hurt my mouth too. . . . (Oh, he's mad! . . . Good God! He's gone clean crazy! He's panting and neighing and snorting and plunging and kicking up a row! My God! what a row! He's mad, quite mad! Fancy doing a kick up when one's drawing a carriage in a first class show!)"

Nero did indeed appear to have gone quite mad : he panted and quivered and pawed the ground, neighing and squealing. The lackeys sprang hastily down from their carriage to hold him— they had just reached the door of the palace where they were due to halt, where they were received by a large company of gentlemen, all very trim, in frock coats and silk hats.

"What's happened?" everyone was asking. "Oh, look! look! One of the horses is playing up!"

They rushed up, surrounding the hearse in a jostling crowd and watching the proceedings with interest and surprise, some of them shocked and frightened. The servants were unable to control Nero. The coachman stood up and tugged furious

ly at the reins, but all in vain. The horse continued to paw the ground, neighing and trembling
violently, with his head turned towards the door-
way of the palace.

He only quieted down when an aged servant in
livery emerged from that door-way, pushed the
lackeys on one side and caught hold of the reins.
Recognising the animal at once, he cried out with
tears in his eyes:—

"Why, it's Nero! it's Nero! Poor old Nero! Of
course he is excited . . . he was our dear mistress'
horse! The horse of the poor princess! He
recognises the palace, you know . . . he smells his
stable. Poor Nero! . . . come, be good. Yes, you
can see, it's me, your old Giuseppe. . . . Now
stand still! . . . that's better. . . . Poor old Nero,
you have the task of taking her away—d'you see?—
your old mistress, whom you still remember . . .
it's your duty to convey her. She'll be glad it's you
who are to take her for her last drive."

Furious at the discredit brought upon the under-
taker's firm—with all those gentlefolk present, too
—the driver was still pulling savagely at the reins
and threatening to flog the horse, but Giuseppe
called out to him:—

"That'll do! That'll do! Stop it! I'll look after
him . . . he's as quiet as a lamb. . . . Sit down.
I'll lead him the whole way. . . . We'll go together
—eh, Nero?—taking our kind mistress, very

quietly, as we always did, eh? You'll be good, so's not to hurt her, won't you? . . . Poor old Nero! You still remember her, don't you? They've shut her up in the big box and now they're just carrying her down. . . ."

At this point Fofo, who had been listening from the other side of the shaft, was so astonished that he broke in with the enquiry:—

"Inside the box!—your mistress?"

Nero launched a kick sideways at him.

But Fofo was too excited by his new discovery to resent the attack:—

"Oh! I see! Now I see! So we . . ." he went on to himself, "so we . . . I mean to say . . . Yes, of course, I've got it now! . . . That old man's weep⸗ing. . . . I've often before seen lots of others weep on similar occasions . . . so often seen long faces, sad faces . . . and heard sad music . . . just like now. . . . Yes, now I know all about it. . . . That's why our job's such a soft one! It's only when men must weep, that we horses can be happy and have a restful time . . ."

He felt strongly tempted to do some kicking and prancing on his own account.

JAN